Masterminds

T Berry Jones

Published by FastPencil Publishing

Second Edition

http://fp.fastpencil.com

Printed in the United States of America

Table of Contents

For my two sisters who love cracking codes,

my problem solving mother,

and my father who always loves a good adventure.

❧

CHAPTER 1

Chapter 1

Rose hopped along the stones, refusing to look back. She continued to run, having no intention of where she was going. She only knew one word. *Away.*

She continued to run through the woods that she had played in countless times before her sixth birthday. The last time she joyfully frolicked in the woods was three years ago, and she had a difficult time remembering where her favorite hiding tree was. Once it seemed as if she was running in circles, Rose stopped, and quickly scaled a tree. She looked as far as her small eyes could see. In all directions, she saw nothing but trees and forest. She turned to look around again when she heard a subtle crack, but it was loud enough to send chills of fright through her body. Was that her tree? Or the enormous one next to her? Rose scrambled off of her branch, sliding back down the tree. She tumbled to the ground, landing with a thump. She bounced back up, running again, trying to leave the area before the whole tree went down.

Still overcome with fear and shock, Rose tripped on a root. She steadied her breath and tried to rub the dirt off of her body. She got to her feet and looked around. Rose found another tree, but was scared to climb it. What if there was a fungus that spread in the forest that made the trees frail? Then she remembered what her father had told her about the trees.

"Some of them are young and strong, like you," he had said, "but others are old and weak."

"Like you!" Rose had replied.

"Hey!" Her father laughed. "I just want you to know that if you hear a crack, you run like the wind. Got it?"

"Got it."

The mammoth tree next to the one she was climbing must have been old, and could have fallen down on top of her. It wasn't going to happen again.

Recalling her conversation with her dad allowed her to build the confidence to climb another tree. When she got to the top, in the far distance, the town was visible. The town where her father used to work. The town she had never been allowed to visit since.

Rose excitedly climbed back down the tree and ran towards the town. Occasionally, she climbed another tree to make sure she was headed in the right direction. After lots of running and climbing, the town was visible from the ground. The trees slowly turned into houses, the dirt turning to stone walkways.

A young man saw her and turned the other way. Rose looked down at her torn clothes. She was a mess, but that was the least of her concerns. An older woman caught sight of her, and her eyes widened with shock.

"Are you- You couldn't be young Hillary!" she exclaimed.

"No, I'm Rose."

"You undeniably look like your father." The woman took Rose's hand but she struggled away. She didn't trust this woman.

The woman did not give up. She had surprising strength for what seemed like an old age. She grabbed Rose Hillary by the waist and carried the young girl over her shoulder. She walked into her small clothing shop and set Rose in a very tall chair. It must have been some type of adult sizing chair where even their feet weren't supposed to touch the ground.

Rose's legs dangled in the air and she kicked them furiously. For the moment, she didn't take any immediate action, but she could jump down onto the hard floor if she really had to.

"Your father worked in the building next door. He was... an engineer, darling."

Rose stared at her blankly.

"Someone who makes things better. Anyway, last week I received a letter in my mailbox here at the shop, and it was addressed to RH. I thought that meant Roger Hillary, but uh, I haven't seen him for years."

"Three."

She ignored Rose's correction. "Now I know it's addressed to you! Rose Hillary. Here ya go. Don't lose it, dear." She handed the envelope to Rose. "Now what brings ya out here, darling? I thought Roger lived on the other side of the woods."

Rose stubbornly stared into space.

"No? Well, who're you with now?"

Rose refused to respond. Three years ago her father got an opportunity for a better job elsewhere. Rose was only six then, and her father thought that it was best for her to stay where she was. Rose was forbidden to explore the woods and visit the town like she used to do with her father, because her mother missed him too much. After three years of no adventures, Rose was eager to explore the world. She was nine now, and decided that she would somehow find her father. She would use her quickness, her agility and all her athleticism to find new adventures and soar new heights. Somehow she would find a way to make her father proud.

"I guess I best be sending you home, dearie. But first why don't you warm up with a cup of tea and a cookie."

Nothing.

"I'm just trying to help."

"I don't need any," Rose snapped. With that, she leaped off the extremely tall chair and hit the floor, hard. She popped up and ran off with the envelope in hand. Away from the town. Away from the woods. Away from her boredom and captivity.

Thunder rumbled. The wind blew furiously. Rose watched the sky grow dark. She stopped running only to catch her breath, but then saw the unopened letter, sitting in her hand. She was hesitant to open it, coming from a stranger. It started to drizzle. She hid under the umbrella of a tree, and temptation outweighed her doubt. What if it was about her father? She needed to know. Just as she tore off the envelope, lightning struck the tree above her. Rose shrieked and sprinted away, now exposed to the rain. It fell faster and heavier. Rose didn't care about getting drenched, she just wanted to get to safety. With the letter in one hand, and the envelope in the other, Rose ran as fast as she could. As she was running, a gust of wind blew the letter out of her hand. The storm surged on, and Rose was left in the open. And possibly even worse, her empty envelope would never reveal what that letter said.

~

CHAPTER 2

Chapter 2

John examined the letter one more time. He had received it in the mail from his school principal, Mr. Toro. He was in trouble, again. John had been tapping morse code on the table during his History teacher's lecture. When Mr. Holland had ordered him to stop, John had replied, "How else will the robbers know that this is the wrong class to burst into? It's too boring!" The class had burst out laughing, and John got out of his seat. He crouched behind the desk, and jumped out using his hands to make a gun. He pointed it at his friend Robby and ordered him to put his hands up and give him all of his money.

The entire class thought the spoof was hysterical (well maybe not Susanna Luckran; she was too engrossed in the history of Ancient Rome.) However, Mr. Holland wasn't okay with that comment. He gave John an intense glare and motioned for John to follow him into the hall. As he went to open the door, he jumped back at the sight of Carl and Joe, two of the star players from the legendary school basketball team, sticking their tongues out with their faces pressed against the glass of the classroom door.

John, Carl, and Joe, were all in trouble with the principal, and had all received discipline letters.

Now, as John ran his hands over the soft parchment, he flipped it over to the back. There was an identical header and footer at the top and bottom of the page as on the front, like there was supposed to be something present. But there was nothing. He slid his hands up and down the paper, and discovered stiff, crusty areas, that he didn't notice from the beginning.

"Marta!" he shouted up the stairs.

His twin sister Marta was not looking forward to whatever joke John was about to tell her. "What?" She yelled from her station at the computer.

"Come down! I have something to show you! It's my letter from the principal!"

She sighed and started walking down the stairs. "John, what did you do this time?"

Marta went over to the kitchen counter where he stood with the letter. He didn't say anything. He just passed her the paper, and by the look on his face alone, she knew something was up. When John was really excited his face would light up, and a shade of emerald green would twinkle in his normally hazel eyes. He had discovered something about the letter. She disregarded the message about discipline and consequences on the front that she'd seen many times before on John's other letters, and flipped the paper over to the back.

He grabbed the paper back from her and almost ripped it with his excitement. "Invisible Ink! On the back of the letter from the principal of school!!!!"

"No way! Let me see!" Marta tore the paper from her brother's hands and examined the back. "Let's heat it up to activate the ink." They ran up the stairs, John almost tackling Marta in the process. They rushed to her desk, where she held the paper under her reading lamp. The lamp produced so much light and heat, the hidden message appeared almost right away.

What you have done, I find comical. What you will do, is a mystery. Come where the act was performed and do not be late. ~ Noa Nysoum

"Whoa." John was fascinated.

"Who is Noa Nysoum?"

"Don't know," John replied.

Silence enveloped the room as the twins thought about the mysterious message.

Finally, Marta broke the silence. "So... are you going?"

"Going where?"

"Mr. Holland's classroom," Marta stated.

"What?" John was disappointed now.

"'The place where the act was performed,' you know, like the place where you catapulted you pencil across the room?"

John smiled. "Actually, this time it was morse code to signal Carl and Joe, the basketball prodigies from our school. The door was locked and they were trying to get in, and I used morse code to signal them to leave this boring class while they could, but instead it brought Mr. Holland over to them and uh, got us all in the doghouse."

"For tapping on a desk?"

"Well, I um, kinda mentioned robbers, and-"

"Robbers? John, you know how he thinks about them," she teased. It was true though, Mr. Holland was especially strict about the subject of robbers and criminals breaking into the school. John wondered if it had happened before, but Mr. Holland refused to talk about it.

"Yeah, I know. But anyway, I guess I'll be seeing the basketball hotheads in his room for detention. Boy, I was expecting like,'I'm sorry I've been such a terrible principal so I'm inviting you and your lousy sister to an ice cream party.'"

"I have to say you got me excited, too. Well, we'd better get you there."

Marta left a note for their parents, who were both at work, and followed John to the garage. They put on their helmets and she rolled her bicycle out to the driveway. John found his skateboard in a pile of sports equipment, and they left the house in a hurry. On the way, John imagined the endless possibilities of the invisible ink letter containing any other message, besides what was actually there. He could have been on his way to an enormous truck of video games or a super fun skateboarding contest, or a big make-your-own ice cream sundae buffet. But instead, he was on his way to a boring and usual detention as a consequence for his senseless action.

When they arrived at the school, Ms. Shyrra, their strict secretary, was exiting the building. Her head swiveled side to side, searching for her car in the parking lot. They were guaranteed to be spotted shortly. Marta went to hide behind the school walls. John, on the other hand, did not cower from their secretary, and was only concerned about their way in. With her back turned toward them, she recalled that her car was parked out front. As she was walking away, John kicked his skateboard out from under him and it went flying towards the door. As it closed, the skateboard was there to stop it from closing and locking. It was a good plan, but the force of the heavy door and the rolling wheels on the skateboard caused it to roll past the door and into the school. The door slammed shut, locking John and Marta outside, and John no longer had his skateboard.

A car engine whirred to a start, and John joined Marta behind the school walls. The last thing they wanted was to be spotted and caught by Ms. Shyrra. She would give you detention for a week just for glaring at her.

When her car drove away, Marta and John emerged from their hiding spot. "Way to go, genius," Marta snapped.

"Hey, it's not like you did anything better," he mumbled back. John stuffed his hands in his pockets, and kicked a rock. "Do you think we can get in through the front?"

"Ms. Shyrra is always the last person to leave after school. All of the doors are locked now."

"Aww man, that means we missed the video game truck that Principal Toro was going to give us!! He must be gone, too."

They were as hopeless as two refugees stranded on a remote island.

John stared at the shiny cars in the parking lot, scanning his brain for a plan. As he continued to think, he wondered why there were still some cars in the parking lot.

"Marta, the cars! There must be people here!" John exclaimed.

Just as he came to the conclusion, Carl and Joe poked their heads out the gym door. Sweat dripped down their faces, and splashed down, landing on John's skateboard. Carl was holding a basketball, and Joe was sliding John's yellow skateboard back and forth underneath his foot.

"Hey, that's mine!" John shouted, diving for his skateboard.

Joe kicked the skateboard backwards. Carl laughed at the look on John's face. "It's John, right?" Carl asked, staring down at John who continued to sit on the sidewalk. "You won't get your skateboard back without..." he paused, searching for the right word.

"Paying. For the trouble you got us into." Joe finished.

John swallowed. They were tough, strong, relentless basketball players. And he was weak. But he wasn't going to let them see his fear.

"Hey, guys, relax. My sister and I only came back for our uh, reward. From Principal Toro. I'm pretty sure he wanted you guys to come, too."

"What kind of reward?" Joe had a skeptical tone in his voice, but Carl seemed very interested.

"He didn't tell me. I think it's a surprise. Maybe ice cream, video games, sword fighting, basketball?"

Now they were fully on board. John successfully used his worm to catch the fish. "C'mon in." Carl offered.

Joe grabbed the yellow skateboard and handed it to John.

"Thanks."

Carl entered the gym and explained his understanding of the situation to his basketball coach. "Me and Joe have a two on two basketball tourney for Principal Toro. See ya tomorrow at practice!" And with that, Carl, Joe, John, and Marta walked down the hall to Mr. Holland's room.

"You'd best be tellin' the truth, bud." Joe warned.

They peered through the glass of the door. The lights were out, and no one was inside.

Joe was about ready to punch John. "Are we supposed to play basketball in his classroom? Huh? Why'd you take us here?!!"

John hid his cherry colored face and tried the door. Surprisingly, it opened with ease, exposing them to a dark and vacant classroom. All of the desks were pushed against the walls, but Principal Toro- or whoever was supposed to be there- was gone. Basketballs, footballs, soccer balls, skateboards, baseballs, scooters, balance beams and wrestling mats, everything John could have imagined, surrounded the room. Carl and Joe ran over to the basketballs and started playing one vs. one. Before John grabbed the baseball, Marta grabbed his shirt and pulled him back.

"There must be something strange going on here. Help me look around," she whispered privately to John. They scanned the room for traps or clues. She noticed a fading envelope on one of the desks. It was labeled M+J. As she picked it up, she jumped backwards. A spider!! She shrieked as it fell to the floor. Tentatively, Marta kicked it with her foot and it slid across the floor, not flinching at all. It normally should have flailed it's limbs. Marta was afraid of spiders, but this one was odd. It must be dead. She called John over to squash it with a kleenex. He picked it up, but it leaped out of his hand. Marta shrieked again. John laughed at her and stomped on the spider. It crunched and sparked, creating a very low drone that dropped into silence.

"It was a bug," he said.

"Really genius?? A bug. How profound," Carl jeered.

Joe was equally unimpressed. They continued to play and make fun of John at the same time. Marta looked over at John. She knew what he was talking about. Mr. Holland's classroom was being bugged. Someone was trying to listen in on the conversation.

After their basketball showdown, Carl and Joe finally noticed the envelope Marta was examining. Joe pointed to the door and shouted, "Mr. Holland's coming!" Marta and John looked up to the door in panic. Carl jumped up and stole the envelope right out of her hands, and the two of them ran out the door. Too engrossed in the curiosity brought by the letter, they ran straight into a janitor who was cleaning the hall, knocking over his soapy water bucket. The athletic boys leaped over the water, dropping the letter into the suds. The letter absorbed the water, causing all of the ink to run and blur.

John felt ashamed for falling for such a foolish trick, but chased after them to try and retrieve the letter. He ran straight into the puddle and slipped, but Marta was at the door, holding his skateboard. She tossed it to him, he caught it, and he grabbed the soggy letter. John hopped on the skateboard and together, the twins exited the building. Marta had a hunch that they would have gotten what they needed, but it was ruined. She retrieved her bike from the rack, and they set off for home. The muscular boys were long gone, in their cars riding home. Their parents were here to pick them up from basketball practice, so they left like nothing had happened. But they were everything but right.

~

Chapter 3

"Are we supposed to play basketball in his classroom? Huh? Why'd you take us here?!!"

Tim jumped out of his skin at the sudden noise, wondering what could have caused it. But soon he realized exactly what was going on. The bug he had placed in the middle school for his current events project was working! Just like he knew it would. *But why would it be going off now? It's evening; no one should be in school now! This will skew all of the data I took for the past two weeks! I knew Mr. Holland's classroom was not a good place to put my bugs, but it was the only room left! All of the other students got to choose a teacher's classroom on the day I was in the national computer programming competition!! It was Mr. Sullivan's fault anyway, for assigning us to visit and explore the environment at the middle school in the first place,* Tim reflected.

But then he thought about the significance of the comment that he had heard. It seemed awfully strange. And intriguing. Tim decided to turn up the volume and listen in, hoping to discover something exciting.

Suddenly, a shrill, high pitched scream caused Tim to nearly fall out of his seat. After regrouping and straightening his thick glasses, Tim realized that he most definitely recognized the voice that had created the shriek. He racked his brain and quickly recalled who it was: Marta Ivanson. He went to robotics camp with her this past summer, and he was eager to find out what she was up to now.

As he listened in more closely, he heard a crunch, static, a low drone, then silence.

Hey! They destroyed my bug! Oh well. They think I only have one? Ha! Tim grabbed another bug from his bucket. This time it was a ladybug. His initial intention was to replace the broken spider in Mr. Hollands classroom, but decided that he had plenty of data to complete his project. Now he had another project on his hands.

He quickly searched his school directory for the twins' address, but he was unsuccessful. *Duh, Tim, they're still at the middle school!* He smacked himself on the forehead and searched for the middle school address book. He found it and went straight to the highlighted address. Tim set the ladybug on the passenger's seat and turned on his black van. He would have to save his convertibles and sports cars for later. This mission required an inconspicuous vehicle. He didn't want to be noticed driving an expensive car at an average house. Tim plugged the address into the newest phone model and used it as a GPS.

Ten minutes later, Tim arrived at the Ivanson's house. He tried the front door. Of course it was locked. Tim set the ladybug in the bushes and would use his remote controller to direct it inside when the twins got home.

Just as Tim was patting himself on the back, he heard the small ring of a bicycle bell. Marta was close, probably John too. He needed to get out of there.

~

Marta and John came from the back road and entered through the garage right before a black van recklessly drove away. Marta was too focused on the mysterious letter, and thought nothing of it. She recalled the initials on the front of the letter: M+J. It must have been addressed to Marta and John. She was so sure it would have contained a secret message that coded into some form of punishment for the comedy that John had performed. But now, they wouldn't know what it said, and John would get in even more trouble from the principal for not doing his punishment.

John couldn't get the picture of the spider out of his head. "Who put it there, and why would they want to bug us?" he finally asked.

"I'm not really sure. Someone had to be controlling it, though. Remember? It jumped out of your hands right before you crushed it."

"What about the letter?" John tried.

"It's ruined. We'll never know what it said," Marta responded hopelessly.

"Let me see." John took the letter. He opened it up and unfolded the two pieces of paper that were folded to fit into a small envelope. He only ripped the creases even further. Eighteen pieces fluttered to the ground. John left the room, grunting and went to go play a videogame. Marta cleaned up John's mess, putting the pieces on her desk. If they were ever going to look at them, they would be more effective dry.

Marta pulled her math worksheet out of her binder and zipped through the problems, but couldn't keep her mind off of the letter. She closed her binder after finishing the assignment. Then, she went back to the torn pieces. They were still damp, but able to be worked with. She spread the pieces out on the floor, and investigated. The ink was extremely too blurry to comprehend, and was almost like a shooting star streaking across the pages. She picked one up and it drooped in her hand. She turned it around until the blurred words resembled something like the letter "d." The next one she picked up was round, but not exactly circular. It resembled a letter "o." She continued to find hidden letters in the pieces of paper. She found a "u" an "m" and another "o." The next letter she picked up was blank. It had no ink on it whatsoever. Marta set it down and continued to interpret the hidden message. The remaining pieces spelled out "lift echoes" with another blank card.

"John!" She called.

He came running down the stairs. "Did you find the ice cream?"

"What?"

"Oh, sorry."

"I found something in the blurred remains of the letter." She showed him her array of small papers with large blurry letters on them.

“Whoa.”

“The words blurred together and formed bigger letters. Do you think it means something??”

“I don’t know. It seems too odd to be a coincidence.” John looked at Marta. “May I?”

She nodded.

John picked up a few of the pieces and slid them around. He grabbed a fresh piece of paper and scribbled down some combinations.

u doom lift echoes

school die fume toe

dome flies hoot cue

“But what about the blank pieces?” Marta questioned, noticing that he had left those aside.

“Oh yeah,” John mumbled. “I forgot.”

“Could they be spaces? That limits us to three words!”

“Okay, I’ll try it I guess.”

feld heist Mooceou

come to fieldhouse

“Feld heist mooceou? What’s that?” Marta asked.

“I don’t know. Maybe feld means failed, and Mooceou is a place? Some-one failed a heist in Mooceou?”

Marta disapprovingly glared at John. He crossed it off of his list. “That leaves come to fieldhouse.”

~

CHAPTER 4

Chapter 4

"Come to fieldhouse, eh? What fieldhouse?" Tim said aloud. His ladybug was working. He could hear Marta Ivanson very clearly. Now he wanted to upgrade his bugs and add a camera so that he could see her just as clearly. He hadn't seen her dazzling eyes and brown hair since last summer at the robotics camp. Now, he had a feeling that they would see each other again. At the fieldhouse.

Tim explored his internet database and searched "fieldhouse." In a fraction of a second, about 5 million results popped up. How would he find the right one? He clicked through the first page of results, not satisfied with any of them. Tim yawned as he scrolled through, staring at the bright white screen. His head drooped past his arm and onto the desk as he snored in deep slumber.

He was in a hallway with bouncy red floors, divided into six lanes by white stripes. Tim continued to walk until he spotted a white number on the ground. It wasn't a hallway, it was a track. It extended around in an oval, the size of a regular track. Tim searched for a way out, but ended up walking around in circles. There were walls on both the inside and outside of the track, but he couldn't find any doors. Was he trapped? Tim walked around the track again, and came to the same conclusion. He stopped at the white numbers on the track, and a crazy idea formed in his mind. If he jumped on the six numbers in the right order, maybe he would escape. He did the quick math in his head. There were only 720 combinations. He began trying them at once. After what seemed like three hours, the ground rumbled. He was lifted off of his feet, spinning and rising. The world around him grew black and all he could see was darkness. Only then Tim realized his eyes were closed. He forced them open to get a better look, and found himself in the upstairs room in his house filled with high tech computers. He must have fallen asleep last night. His hours of hard work were only a dream. But he still remembered it clearly.

Tim glanced at the clock and reality slapped him in the face. Today was Friday, and he had school. In his haste, Tim stumbled over the keyboard and the screen flashed awake to the page about fieldhouses. Remembering his dream, Tim quickly added six numbers to the search bar. fieldhouse, 5 2 4 1 3 6. It took him directly to a page, then blacked out. A notification popped up.

You do not have permission to view this site. Please scan your envelope here.

After a few seconds, Tim was directed to the camera. He was alarmed to see his disheveled hair, crooked glasses, and his clothes from yesterday, once again reminding him that he needed to get ready for school. As embarrassing as the image was, Tim screenshotted the notification, web address, and unfortunately, the camera screen. He shut down and locked his computer database and hurried into his bedroom to get ready for school.

~

Carl dribbled the basketball down the court and shot a three pointer. He flicked his wrist finishing high as the ball swished through the netting of the basket.

"He shoots, he scores! Three points to win his team the championship. Carl! Carl!" He cheered, mocking his best friend, Joe.

They were playing one on one basketball in the gym before school started that morning and Carl just barely beat out Joe when the first bell, the warning bell, rang. Since he was winning, Carl decided that it was time to stop. In frustration, Joe dribbled down the court and slam dunked it into the basket. Just as they were collecting their things, their coach entered the gym.

"Hey boys!" He shouted. "If it's alright with you, I have a few things to tell you before you go off to class."

"Sure, man!" Carl replied, eager to miss as much school as possible.

"Okay great." Their coach closed his eyes and they could see that he was deeply thinking. He looked quite confused. He slowly opened his eyes and started to talk. "You two are the best players on my- our team. Someone told me- I mean I heard about a one vs. one tourney. I want you two to represent our school. Will you do it?"

The two boys looked at each other with beaming grins.

"Oh yeah!" Carl shouted.

"We're in," nodded Joe.

"Great!" The confused look wiped off of his face and was replaced with excitement.

"Just one thing man. Where and when is it?" Carl asked.

The confusion returned on the coach's face and he tried to remember the valuable information. "fieldhouse 5241 something something at 8:00 Saturday (tomorrow) morning. Thanks boys!"

~

Rose woke up underneath a park bench. She was drenched and terrified, but alive. The storm had stopped, yet the sky was still a dreary and ominous gray. She didn't have the letter anymore, but the empty envelope made the desire to see her father increase. Then her thoughts moved away from her father, and settled on food. Her stomach was an erupting volcano.

Motivated by food and curiosity, Rose emerged from underneath the bench and set off through the trees. After a while she scaled one, and spotted a path not far from her. She swung down and ran on to it. She started walking again, not having the slightest idea of where she was going.

~

"Timothy, I said, will you please read the passage on atoms!?" The class groaned. They hated it when Tim read because he was a geek who made them all seem dumb.

Tim snapped out of his thoughts and realized that Mr. Kallipio had called on him.

"Sorry," he mumbled. Then he began to read what seemed like a preschool level passage on atoms, adding a few college level scientific words to make the passage more interesting.

After his science class came English, then he had a break for lunch. Tim couldn't focus on his school work, because his mind was too focused on his dream. He decided there was one thing to do. He forced himself to push through a normally thrilling school day. When it was over, Tim left his Jeep in the highschool parking lot, strolled out of the building and walked on the sidewalk to the middle school across the street. He needed to set a few things straight.

The middle school still had an hour of school left, so he needed to be inconspicuous. He walked around to the side door where trucks came to make deliveries. He crouched behind a bush as the delivery man exited the building whistling, and started the truck. He drove off and Tim caught the door before it closed and locked. Tim dragged along the walls as he walked through his old school. He couldn't remember it very well, but could at least remember how to get to Mr. Holland's classroom from his location. He ran up the stairs, skipping every other step, and passed two doors on the right. *Drat! He's teaching right now! How will I get an envelope from him?* Tim stopped before passing the open door. He didn't want to be seen. *Wait a minute. Mr. Holland NEVER left his door open. I remember that much. He must have a substitute.* Tim went back downstairs and went to the cafeteria. He cracked open the door to the teacher's lounge and was relieved to find it empty. Tim strolled in and saw a vending machine filled with snacks and drinks. There was a coffee machine and a crumb cake sitting on the counter. Tim cut himself a piece and was careful to clean up every last crumb he dropped after stuffing the desert in his mouth. Then he saw what he was looking for: The teacher's mailboxes.

Mr. Holland's section had a few letters in it, proving that he was most likely absent today. Tim went through them, but didn't find anything worthwhile. Disappointed, Tim exited the lounge and walked back to his Jeep. Tim started it up and drove home, perplexed about how he could get his envelope, or if he even had one.

~

Chapter 5

Eventually, Rose arrived at a small area with big houses, sidewalks, bike paths and beautiful yards. She walked along the sidewalks, internally battling herself to knock on a door and ask for food and directions. But she was too scared.

Suddenly, a loud voice startled her.

"On your left!" The young boy shouted as he passed on his skateboard.

"Excuse us, sorry," the girl apologized she started to pass on her bike.

Rose's curiosity, and need for kind people beat out her fear. She tried to grab the back of the girl's blue bike. "Wait!" She commanded.

The girl stopped pedaling and braked. "Yeah?"

Rose took a deep breath. "I don't exactly know where we are right now, and I haven't eaten in a day. I'm not expecting you to do anything." Rose realized that she was holding out the envelope, so she hid it behind her back.

But Marta saw the girl trying to hide an envelope behind her back. "I'm Marta. I wonder if you could possibly show me what's behind your back? I can get you some food, and maybe a pair of dry clothes."

Rose slowly nodded and held out the envelope. "I'm Rose."

John jumped his skateboard off of the curb and turned around to find Marta. *She probably stopped to talk to the red headed girl on the sidewalk. Yep. There she is.* He skated closer.

"Hi, John!" Rose shouted.

"What? How do you know me? We're not cousins are we?" John looked at Rose more closely, trying to decide if he had seen her before.

"Relax, John. This is Rose. She was lost in the storm last night." She flashed him the envelope. "We're going to show her the map at home," she winked.

"Okay. Cool with me. See you sloths there!" John flipped his skateboard and took off way ahead of them. Rose glared at Marta, warning her not to do the same, but Marta simply returned the gesture with a compassionate smile, never pulling ahead.

When they arrived at the house, John had sandwiches, potato chips, the letter and the secret message laid out for them. Rose was impressed with her new friends' hospitality. For many years, she had been isolated in her cottage, alone with her mother, longing for friends and adventures, and now here she was, ready to explore the world.

"We got a letter just like yours. The handwriting on the envelopes was identical." Marta explained as she recalled her and John's envelope before it was dropped into the soapy suds. The characters were at the same angle, had the same curve, and were the same size.

"Which means that the hidden information in yours is the same as ours." John skeptically glanced at Marta, silently asking if it was okay to reveal the info.

She nodded. "Come to fieldhouse. That's all we know so far. But there are others involved. Us. You. Two basketball players named Carl and Joe. And- and maybe others."

~

Noa Nysoum toured the fieldhouse one last time, inspecting each difficult challenge. He and his team straightened up the building , making sure it was perfectly ready for the teams to arrive. But he already knew that his fieldhouse was ready. The real question was: Were the teams ready for the upcoming tests? The rooms were structured correctly, containing the essential items that correspond with the challenge. The hidden cameras were stationed properly. The teams were notified, but the rest was to be determined. Who will show up? Who won't get past the first task? Who will quit? Who will be victorious? Noa Nysoum loved every unknown aspect that this entire event required. He just couldn't wait to get it started.

Noa Nysoum thought about the competitors he informed. Did that idiot coach tell his players the information he was given? Did the sketchy woman in the town find the red headed girl? Did the anxious teacher remember to give the twins their letter? He relied on too many people to do the job for him. That just made it even more mysterious.

~

Tim typed the same URL address into the search bar on his database. The same notification popped up, directing him to the camera to scan his envelope. He combed his fingers through his hair, knowing what he had to do. He needed to know what that website was about. He needed an envelope. And that meant he needed Marta. Tim grabbed his shades and the keys to his sports car. This mission required stealth, but also speed. He whizzed out of his gated driveway and down the road. He drove to the same place he had let loose his ladybug, but stopped three houses down the road, where uncontrolled and overgrown bushes blocked his car from sight. Tim pulled out the controls to his ladybug. He didn't know exactly where it was, but he directed it around the house until he heard voices.

Yep. They're home! Time to initiate phase two. Tim smirked and prepared his secret weapon. Something he'd been working extremely hard on ever since last summer. He pulled out his magnificently important miniscule ant. With camera settings. And the ability to pick things up. He set the ant on the grass and turned on his ipad. The bush next to him appeared on the large screen. It was working.

Tim directed the ant over to the house and scanned it. *Bingo.* An upstairs window was ajar. The ant climbed up the brick wall and squeezed through the open window. Tim hit the yellow scan button again. No one was in the room. It was junky and unorganized with clothes scattered everywhere, and monster posters covering the walls. *Must be the boy's room. John, is it? Let's get out of here. Marta wouldn't leave an important envelope with her messy twin brother.*

The ant crawled under the crease of the closed door and down the hall. Tim watched his screen until another room appeared on the right. He moved the joystick into the room and hit the scan button. Tim jumped out of his seat as an alarm blared.

Alert! Alert! People in area! Quantity 3.

3? Who's the third? Tim looked around the room. Sure enough, there stood Marta, John, and a very small red headed girl. Papers were scattered around the room, and Tim zoomed in closer. The one in John's hand had many random combinations of words. The last phrase was circled.

Come to fieldhouse.

This is it! It must be here somewhere.

Tim continued to control the ant's field of vision, darting from wall to wall. He closely examined each paper on the ground and on the desk. Then he moved back to the unknown red headed girl. *Who is she? And what is in her hand?*

Tim swiveled back to the paper in her hand and zoomed in. It was an envelope. *The* envelope. He snapped a picture and it appeared on the ipad screen. *Mission success!* Just in case he would need to access the twin's house again, he maneuvered the ant into a corner underneath a cardboard box.

Tim tried to contain his excitement until his car was out of sight. "Wohoo!" he shouted once out of the neighborhood.

Tim dragged the image onto a blank envelope template and printed it. He sucked in a deep breath and went to the fieldhouse website. The same notification popped up.

You do not have permission to view this site. Please scan your envelope here.

"Oh yes I do!" Tim exclaimed.

Tim held up the freshly printed envelope with the letters RH on the front. The screen flashed red and another message appeared.

For all of you frauds, thieves, and hackers, you can not outsmart the wit of our tech people here at fieldhouse 5 2 4 1 3 6. That is not a valid envelope.

"Arg!" Tim grunted. An image wouldn't suffice. He needed the real thing.

Having no time to lose, Tim grabbed the keys to the same red sports car and took off. Just as he was about to pull in the same driveway three houses down, the car in front of him pulled in. Someone would surely notice him there, and the car filled the driveway space anyway.

Tim tried four houses down, but the bugs and the remotes were too far out of range. He was forced to deal with the house two away from the twins.

"Alright Antie, what's the status?" Tim asked as he fired up the controls. The screen blinked on, and to his pleasant surprise, no one was in the room. Tim moved the ant around the room, looking for the envelope. The ant crawled up the desk, and there it was, sitting there. *How could I be so lucky?* Tim pressed the purple button and tapped the envelope. The ant crawled underneath it and lifted it with ease. The ant moved twice as slow, but managed to cross the room towards the window. The ant walked up the wall, and crawled out the window. Tim jerked the controls but the ant dropped the envelope as it crashed to the ground. His screen flickered off and he could hear static from the audio.

"Not good. Not good!" Tim smacked his hand on the dashboard in frustration. He didn't have any more advanced bugs and would have to finish the job himself.

Tim got out of the car and crouched down low. He stayed out of the view from the house and slowly duck walked his way to the driveway. He rolled behind a bush in the front garden and looked around the front yard. No envelope. It must be in the back.

A branch snapped as Tim stood up. He threw himself against the house so that he was directly under the windows, and impossible to see. Tim inched his way around the house and as he looked up he slammed into a heating and air conditioning unit. He felt the nerve in his elbow cause his arm to tingle, and he could feel the sea of purple and blue forming on his knee. Tim ignored his bruises and went around the unit, exposing himself to be seen from the same kitchen window that little Rose just happened to be gazing through.

~

"Ahh!" Rose shrieked.

"What?" John asked.

"Who *is* that?" Rose pointed out the window.

"Is that- could he be Tim Marloy? From robotics camp last summer?" Marta came over to the window as well.

Then everything clicked. The robotic spider from Mr. Holland's classroom. The odd van that pulled out right when they arrived home from school. The bright red sports car John saw leaving.

"Does he drive a bright sports car? I saw one leave earlier today, and there it is again, parked two houses down," John pointed out.

"That's just it. You can't determine if it's him based on his car, because collecting cars is his hobby. But yeah, that car has Tim written all over it," Marta explained.

"But what is he doing here?" Rose accused.

"Let's find out!" John hopped off of the kitchen chair and ran out the front door.

"Wait, John. I have a plan. You go down the driveway and around the house that way. I'll go the other. We'll run into him at some point," Marta directed.

"And what do I do?" Rose asked.

"You can wait by his car in case the tiny chance that we won't run into him occurs," John suggested.

The girls rolled their eyes. "Plan," Rose agreed.

John and Marta each began walking along their side of the house. Though Rose spotted him from the window closer to John's side, Marta was the first to find him outside. She sprinted a few steps forward to catch up to him.

"Hey, Tim! What are you doing here?" Her tone was kind, but she had her suspicions.

~

Tim saw it. There it was. The ticket to knowing what that entire thing was about. The envelope.

"Oh, hi Marta. I was uh, hoping you were home!"

"And why is that?"

"Because, uh." Tim faltered and began to inch toward the envelope, hoping Marta wouldn't see it. "I wanted to ask you a question."

"A question," she raised an eyebrow, but still managed to maintain her kind smile.

"Yeah. Science. You know. School?"

"Oh," Marta sighed. She was slightly disappointed.

"Then why didn't you simply knock on the front door?" John shouted as he neared the others.

"I did! No one answered, so I was going to leave a note in the back." Tim was now two feet from the envelope and an idea struck him. He bent down and grabbed the envelope, making sure to show the side without writing. "See? This is it. I'll read it to you, maybe under some better light?"

John raised the pitch of his voice in mock kindness. "Yes, of course you can come in. Thanks for asking."

"Ignore him," Marta commented as she showed Tim inside. "We can sit here." Marta flicked on the lightswitch, but the lamp didn't turn on.

"Marta, remember? You have to turn-"

"Get a new lightbulb? You're right John! Will you go get it for us?" She elbowed him. Clearly she knew that the knob on the lamp needed to be turned on in addition to the switch on the wall, but she was trying to stall.

"Sure thing," he replied, hopping up the steps.

"We can just move to another room," Tim pointed out.

"No, no. It's okay. He'll be down in a second... but while we're waiting, I have a question for you."

Tim swallowed. Did she realize that the envelope was hers? Or notice it was missing?

"When did you make the spider?" Marta asked calmly.

"What?"

"The robotic spider?"

"Oh. Uh, about that? You're not upset?"

"No, it's okay. It's not like you knew I was afraid of spiders or you were trying to eavesdrop on us." She smiled as her point was enforced.

Tim fiddled with his glasses. He decided to switch the subject. He was beginning to feel guilty, but didn't want his regret to be the cost of the mission.

"I just remembered my question!!" He faked.

"Sorry, Tim, but if *you* don't know the answer, I sure won't. So don't ever use that as an excuse again. I don't know what you're up to, but soon I will!" Marta stormed over to the front door and forcefully swung it open. She practically shoved Tim out the door, and slammed it behind him.

"Well you showed him!" John shouted from the top of the steps.

"Just wait until Rose finds out what he's up to."

~

Tim was confused. He was shocked at how Marta had treated him, yet excited that his mission was a success. He had the envelope!

~

Rose shifted her position from behind the flowers. Her legs were growing tired, and she didn't know what she could do to help anyway. Suddenly, the car headlights blinked and a friendly honk echoed in her ear. The same guy she had seen before just unlocked his car. He had messy hair, thick glasses, a smug look on his face, and an envelope in his hand. With the initials RH on it.

Rose reacted quickly. As he brushed by her flower bed to open the door she stuck out her leg and tripped him. Tim flew down, but caught himself on the cement sidewalk just before a faceplant. The envelope slipped out of his grasp and Rose snatched it. She had it! Now what? She froze there for a few seconds before taking off back to Marta and John's house. She was agile, but Tim picked himself up quickly, and used his longer strides to catch up to her. He managed to grab her left wrist. She knew the other was coming next and the envelope would be gone. She thrust the envelope towards her mouth and clenched it between her teeth. As Tim lunged for her right arm, Rose still had the envelope.

Marta and John came running to the rescue. They had timed their attack perfectly. John reached for the envelope as Rose relaxed her jaw to release her grip. John caught the envelope, wincing as his hand felt a few drops of wet saliva. He wiped it on his shirt and sprinted back towards the house. Marta attempted to shove Tim back to the ground, but he only staggered back a step. Tim ran straight through her towards John, but something landed on his back. The extra weight dragged him, the tight grip around his neck choked him. It was Rose. She was riding Tim piggyback style, with her arms wrapped around his neck holding on until her knuckles grew white. She kicked her legs randomly throwing him off balance. They toppled over and Tim rolled to evenly distribute the impact. He stood up and chased after John. Rose however, didn't get up as quickly. She had slammed against the pavement and pain shot through her body. Rose's vision darkened but she fought it. Marta rushed over to her and helped her sit up. Black and white fireworks danced across her vision, but she continued on back toward the house. Marta and Rose spotted John sitting on the grass, staring at the ground, empty handed. The sound of a car engine starting and tires squealing traveled through the yard. It vibrated loudly in each of their heads, boasting it's great victory.

~

"I can't believe it," moaned John, "What do we do now? Tim has Rose's envelope."

"Does he know that it's empty?" Rose pointed out. The kids burst out laughing. He had nothing but an empty envelope.

~

CHAPTER 6

Chapter 6

But an empty envelope was all he needed.

fieldhouse 5 2 4 1 3 6

Enter

You do not have permission to view this site. Please scan your envelope here.

Camera screen

Tim held up the stolen envelope, the computer scanned it, and snapped a picture. Tim crossed his fingers as he was directed to the original website.

Welcome Hillary, Rose! You have decoded the secret message and discovered this website. Please click below to endure one final test to ensure that you are ready to bear this information, and you are indeed who you say you are.

So that was who the other person was. Rose Hillary. She is about to look very smart.

Tim clicked the button.

List 3 weaknesses + 3 strengths

How am I supposed to know Rose's strengths and weaknesses? Skip.

Why do you want to partake in this challenging event?

That one was easy. Everyone wants to do something to prove their worth. Tim guessed that she wanted to show that she could do anything despite her small size.

What was the secret message concealed in the letter?

Tim thought about what he heard from his bugs, and the significance of the numbers from his dream. He typed "Come to fieldhouse 5 2 4 1 3 6."

Back to the strengths and weaknesses. Tim only met Rose once, and that was 10 minutes ago. Based on her fight to keep her envelope, he assumed that she was determined, quick, and agile, but short, weak, and timid.

Enter

Thank you Rose! Here is your information.

An extreme challenge will take place at fieldhouse 5 2 4 1 3 6 starting at 8:00 on Saturday Morning. Your physical and mental abilities will be tested through difficult tasks. You have the ability to forfeit whenever you feel that you can continue no more, but only the successful team(s) who complete the challenges have the opportunity to join something incredible.

~

The navy blue car Marta easily distinguished as her father's pulled down the driveway and into the garage. She saw John set down his skateboard and run over to greet him. It was getting dark on a Friday night; her mother would pull in shortly.

"Rose?"

Rose looked up from the Harry Potter book Marta let her borrow.

"Our dad is home. Come downstairs and I'll introduce you. I think he can help us."

Reading a few more words, Rose reluctantly put in the bookmark and followed Marta.

"Hi dad! Meet my new friend, Rose! She's helping us with a project."

"Nice to meet you, Rose." He bent down to shake her hand. "I'll let you guys get back to work. Let me know if I can help."

"Okay, thanks dad!"

John put his skateboard away and followed the girls inside. It was too dark to skate anyway.

The three kids gathered in Marta's room. Rose collapsed on Marta's bed and started to read again. John sprawled out on the carpet and Marta sat down at her desk. She went to examine the slips of paper, but needed more light now that the sun set. She switched on her lamp.

"Thanks," Rose mumbled in between sentences. She hadn't noticed that as she was reading, the room had become as dark as an empty cave with flying bats.

"No problem." Marta grabbed a piece with an "o" on it and flipped it over. The heat from the lamp exposed a faint streak of invisible ink. It was the number 2.

"Guys! I found something!" John hopped up and rushed over. Rose kept reading like nothing happened.

More invisible ink numbers formed. They ranged from 1 to 6 and every number was repeated three times. Marta and John put them in order.

1 2 3 4 5 6 1 2 3 4 5 6 1 2 3 4 5 6

"Let's flip them over," John suggested. "It could be telling us the order of the letters."

1 2 3 4 5 6 1 2 3 4 5 6 1 2 3 4 5 6

e o (space) m c t i (space) e f o l u h s o d e

"That's just a bunch of gibberish," Marta commented. "Let's do the opposite. We know the order of the letters, so now we can find out the order of the numbers."

Come to fieldhouse

5 2 4 1 3 6 5 2 4 1 3 6 5 2 4 1 3 6

Rose rolled off the bed and joined them at the desk. Even Harry Potter wasn't as exciting as finding a secret message.

"5 2 4 1 3 6? Does that mean anything to you?" John asked.

"No idea," Rose replied.

"Not to me either," Marta stood up. "Be right back."

"Dad?" Marta shouted.

"What's up?" He replied from the kitchen.

Marta walked down. "Have you ever heard of fieldhouse 5 2 4 1 3 6?"

"No I haven't. But just google it! That's how you kids find out everything else." He pulled out his phone and typed it in.

You do not have permission to view this site. Please scan your envelope here.

"Oh my! Is this a safe site? This project is for school, right?"

"Uh, no. I mean yes! Well, we're not exactly sure. It's a long story starting with Mr. Holland. But we have an envelope from him. That's probably why it's blocked. Just to make sure only his students see it. Thanks, dad."

"Marta? Please be careful okay? You know what mom will say when she gets home."

"Okay." She ran back up the stairs to find John on the same site her father just found, with Rose crowded close by. John held up the blurry envelope with a curious grin, as if asking Marta's permission to scan it.

"It's worth a try!" she concluded with an identical smile.

Welcome Marta and John Ivanson! You have decoded the secret message and discovered this website. Please click below to endure one final test to ensure that you are ready to bear this information, and you are indeed who you say you are.

John began the test.

List 3 weaknesses + 3 strengths

Strengths:

1. good at codes
2. have logical thinking
3. not afraid to take action

Weaknesses

1. clumsy
2. weak
3. melt under pressure

Why do you want to partake in this challenging event?

We are excited to face difficult tasks and solve problems to follow this strange mystery.

What was the secret message concealed in the letter?

Come to fieldhouse 5 2 4 1 3 6

John looked at Marta before submitting their answers. She nodded. They were suitable. He hit enter.

Thank you Marta and John Ivanson! Here is your information.

An extreme challenge will take place at fieldhouse 5 2 4 1 3 6 starting at 8:00 on Saturday Morning. Your physical and mental abilities will be tested through difficult tasks. You have the ability to forfeit whenever you feel that you can continue no more, but only the successful team(s) who complete the challenges have the opportunity to join something incredible.

~

CHAPTER 7

Chapter 7

Joe woke up for the third time to find Carl's dog Sandy panting in his face. He slept over at Carl's house for the big tournament at fieldhouse that morning. He crawled out of his sleeping bag and started the day with 50 pushups and 50 situps. Carl's alarm went off when Joe was already halfway through the push ups, but Carl hopped off his bed and joined him.

Carl's mother was at work, but his father prepared smoothies for the boys before their big day. They gulped them down and jumped into the car, eager to arrive at the basketball tournament they had been anticipating. Carl's father entered the fieldhouse address into his gps and followed the narrow back roads. Though he was skeptical, he continued on. After driving for quite a while, the gps led them to the middle of a cornfield.

"You have reached your destination," the gps chirped before shutting off.

"Oh man," Carl's father muttered as he made a u turn. He drove to the nearest gas station and looked for an old-fashioned map. But fieldhouse 5241 something something wasn't there either. Everyone in the car grunted in frustration. Joe punched the passenger seat which sent Carl flying into the windshield.

"Hey!" Carl complained as he scrambled back into his seat and stared Joe down.

"Whoops," Joe replied coolly.

Carl's father groaned.

They were going to be very late.

~

At 7:45 AM Marta peddled her blue bike faster. She had found coded directions on the site and had solved them with ease, but getting there wasn't so simple. With Rose riding a scooter for the first time and John doing tricks on his yellow skateboard, that left the navigating to her.

The fieldhouse was in the middle of nowhere. They had been riding backroads and trails for 45 minutes and only had 15 minutes left to find it. They powered up a big hill and coasted down, trying to use the speed to push them further. They sped around winding bends and popped wheelies on boulders amid the rocky terrain. Rose almost tipped her scooter of the steep edge of the hill. Eventually, the small path Marta had thought was the trail disappeared and they were lost in a random part of the woods. Rose quickly scaled a tree and her eyes widened with shock. Not far from their location the tree line ended and an enormous building occupied every square inch of visible space. They had found the fieldhouse.

~

Tim had been at the fieldhouse since 7:30. He found it easily because he had been there before. It was only a dream, but he counted it. It was fresh in his mind and seemed real to him. When he had arrived, the front door was surprisingly unlocked and a man who called himself Noa Nysoum welcomed him over a loudspeaker and asked him to wait patiently for the other teams to arrive. Tim was anything but patient. He tapped his foot and bit his fingernails wishing he had his bugs for support. After twenty two minutes, still no one else had arrived. He wondered if he was in the right place, but it was so familiar from his dream.

Finally, Marta, John, and Rose walked in at five minutes till eight, receiving the same greeting as Tim. Two amiable tall girls who Tim had never seen before came in exactly on time. The doors closed with a bang behind them and Noa Nysoum started to explain.

"Welcome to all teams!" belted Noa Nysoum. "Rose... Adella and Marisol... Marta and John... And Tim! Who wasn't even supposed to be here! I never invited him to join us! How he found his way into this challenge is amazing! He was not intended to be included in this big challenge, but somehow he's here and ready to win!"

Noa Nysoum was interrupted by blond haired siblings. The boy was taller and looked to be about three years older than the girl, but they had the same exact face.

"Ah. Eric and Kylie. Nice of you to show up to the fieldhouse," joked Nysoum. "I was just about to explain the rules. You made it just in time."

Eric and Kylie slumped against the wall, sliding to a heap on the ground. Their pale faces turned rosy with embarrassment.

"Each team has the opportunity to participate in many difficult tasks over the course of two weeks. During the weekdays, you will attend school and learn as much as you can to help you through these challenges that will take place on the weekends. Tonight at the appropriate time, I will release you to go back home, and you will return tomorrow morning. Then I will see you again the next weekend. If you tell anyone else about this, you will be thrown out of the competition and for some reason will not recall *anything.* So don't even think about it!

"You must find the locations of the tasks somewhere on fieldhouse grounds, and may choose the order in any way you like. However, if you enter a room with a challenge, you can not leave unless you submit your final answer. Or else you must leave the fieldhouse forever. Your progress will be tracked, and the teams with the most successful records will have the opportunity to join something incredible. Only one team is permitted in a challenge at once, so no joining up, and no copying the team before you. And just remember: We are *always* watching over you."

And with that, Noa Nysoum was off the loudspeaker, stranding the clueless participants in the small room.

"Wow. You'd think that last statement should be reassuring? It was far more creepy," John commented.

No one answered him. After a short spell of silence, whispering between the teams ensued. Each team was developing a complicated plan. Everyone was so engrossed in their own strategizing, no one noticed that Rose used her hair pin to unlock a door, and slipped into another room.

~

Chapter 8

As Rose stepped through the door, she could feel the amount of energy in the room sky rocket. The lights on the ceiling were as bright as the sun on a summer day, and there were fast spinning ceiling fans. But they were on the ground. That was odd.

There were three doors at the other side, but first she needed to get there. Rose found a switch and lowered the fans to the slowest speed, but they were still fast enough to slice into her. She observed the fan's direction. The first was counter clockwise, the second was clockwise, and the third was counter clockwise again. They overlapped slightly and spun like gears. Rose knew it would be easier to go the opposite direction of the fan, so she could jump over each plank.

She used her quick feet to hop through each section of the first fan, then she went the other way through the second. She hopped through the third and just made it out. Only then did she notice that the whole room was sloped down, and the doors were on a higher level. There was a rock climbing wall to get up to the doors. Rose looked around. No harness, no rope. She would just have to do it herself.

Rose reached for the first hand hold but it twisted. There was a loose screw. She tried another, but it was just as unreliable. She found a sturdier one and began to climb, carefully testing each hold before using it. Most of the ones she tried were loose, but she found a few that she could trust to hold her light weight. Rose stretched her small arm to reach a sturdy hold that was just out of her range. Her hand slipped and she immediately panicked. She could feel her face redden with heat, and her heart was racing as she dangled on the climbing wall, staring at the ground far below her. She calmed down and used her feet to inch over and finish her way up the wall.

At the top, Rose wiped her sweaty hands on her shirt, took a deep breath, and picked a door.

~

"Well done, Rose!" Noa Nysoum exclaimed as he watched the video feed and streamed the data from screen 3. Noa Nysoum documented her actions, reactions, and thoughts. He saved his notes on Rose Hillary and looked over at screen 16. The twins were working their way through one of the obstacle courses.

~

"Marta, watch out!" John shouted as a wooden plank whizzed by her head. She ducked just in time. Teams were required to have one person on each path, so John took the high route and Marta was on the low route. John was tip-toeing his way across a rickety suspension bridge that could collapse any second. Marta was crawling through a cylindrical tunnel, right below him. If John fell, he would crush both of them.

Three planks went crashing down as John put a little too much weight on his right foot. His foot fell through, but he caught himself on the side rope. He dangled there for a few seconds, trying to get a better grip with his sweaty hand. His fingers slipped a little as he watched Marta squeeze through the tunnel. She tried climbing on top of it to help John, but it rolled out from underneath her and she toppled over. Despite his own faltering position, he couldn't help laughing at her clumsiness. Marta got up and found one of the planks that John had mistakenly sent down towards her. She threw it up to him and he caught it with his free hand. He placed it on the gap, in the opposite direction of the other planks, so that he could pull himself back up. He cautiously crossed the remainder of the bridge.

His next obstacle was a set of monkey bars. He had plenty of practice with those at his neighborhood park and easily made it across. Marta however, was not a track star, and she had to jump over hurdles. She tripped over the first one and face planted. John stifled his laughter this time. Marta disregarded the scrape on her knee and tried to jump higher the next time. She made it up and over, but she landed on a twisted ankle.

John watched her grimace and heard her small outburst of pain. He wanted to help her, but he didn't know what he could do. He did nothing but watch her slowly stand up and shakily limp over to the next hurdle. John smiled as his brilliant sister climbed under the hurdle instead of over it. He gave her a thumbs up and continued on to a giant twisty slide.

John saluted to Marta even though she wasn't looking in his direction anymore, and shot down the slide. He gained speed as the slide sloped down into a triple twist that almost took him flying off the edge. He was airborne on the double dip and he firmly gripped the edge of the slide to slow his speed. Then John allowed himself to accelerate again on a wide curve that took him outside of the fieldhouse. John went shooting down the final steep slope of the slide and let out an excited whoop as his momentum carried him off the end and into a cargo net. He held on tightly and climbed down where he sat on a rock and waited for Marta to finish.

He thought about how he and Marta ended up in this competition and why Nysoum chose them. They could always leave, but something was driving him forward. Not letting him surrender. Wanting to win.

After what seemed like forever, Marta still hadn't shown up. He could see the end of her path next to his. She had to hop across rocks on a raging river with a swift current traveling back the way they came. John sat on the rock, staring at the river, searching for Marta. But she never came.

"Wooooooaaaaah! Look out below!"

John turned around to see Marta come barreling down the slide and into the cargo net. He helped her stabilize on the ground.

"Are you okay? How did you get to my path?" John noticed her brown hair and clothes were soaked. She was shivering.

"I'm fine I think. I was crossing the river and I slipped off of one of the rocks. I tried to swim against the current and to the end, but I couldn't. It was too strong. So then I swam with the current, hoping it would take me back to the beginning of the obstacle course, which it did! And I went on your path this time, unable to face my downfall again; so here I am!" Marta summed up.

John smiled. He was relieved that she was okay, but a knot formed in his stomach. He knew they had just failed the course.

~

Tim walked into a walk-in-closet sized room with two chairs and a desk. He sat down and picked up one of three papers.

_ 9 2

3 _ 7

8 1 _

—

It was a magic square. Tim expertly filled in the first one.

4 9 2

3 5 7

8 1 6

15

The other two papers were just as easy.

__ 9 16 6

18 _ 13 7

5 15 _ 12

8 14 3 __

__

11 9 16 6

18 4 13 7

5 15 10 12

8 14 3 17

42

16 8 19 __

11 22 _ 17

9 __ 13 20

__ 12 18 6

__

16 8 19 14

11 22 7 17

9 15 13 20

21 12 18 6

57

"As easy as pi!" Tim declared, laughing at his own joke. He slipped the three papers into an answer slot and the door unlocked. Tim left the room feeling confident that he would succeed in all of the challenges. But little did he know, Nysoum had a handful of tricks up his sleeve.

~

CHAPTER 9

Chapter 9

Carl and Joe burst through the fieldhouse door, panting. They were late and lost, but lively.

"We're here for second game!" Carl cried out to an empty room.

"HELLOO!" Joe shouted.

"Hello," a deep voice replied.

Joe jumped and looked around for the source of the voice. But no one was there.

The mysterious voice rang again. "I am Noa Nysoum. And you are-"

"Carl and Joe."

"I was going to say *late.* You are now at a disadvantage because I will NOT explain the rules again. Good luck!" Nysoum mocked.

"Ready Carl?" Joe asked.

"Ready!"

They burst through one of many doors to find themselves in a long, thin stretch of hallway with rainbow checkered tiles. There was a semi-circle of carpet around the door they just walked through, with two pairs of rollerblades sitting on it. All the way at the other end of the hall was another semi-circle shaped carpet.

Carl and Joe sat down and immediately laced up the skates.

"I thought it was a basketball tournament!" Carl accused.

"So did I," Joe sighed disappointedly. But then his usual grin returned as he added, "But hey, I'm not complaining! Roller blading is a good second!"

He finished tying his skates, and he leaned back. His hand slipped off of the carpet and onto the cool tile. A cannon of green paint burst towards him and he somersaulted out of the way. More paint flew towards him, and he jumped over it, landing on the skates. The further he traveled down the hall of rainbow checkered tile, the more paint catapulted towards him.

Carl watched the display of rainbow fireworks around his friend. No paint was aimed at him, so he skated onto the tile. But before he could take another stride, a burst of purple paint splattered the ground in front of him. He swerved around it and speed skated to avoid more paint and caught up to Joe. Carl ducked under a mega burst of red paint. It whizzed past him, hitting directly into Joe.

Carl laughed at his friend. "You look like Elmo on roller blades!" he shouted.

But before he could laugh any more, a wave of ocean blue exploded right before his eyes. And this time he couldn't put it on Joe. He slipped as his feet abruptly stopped in the puddle of sticky paint. He penguin-slid down the hall as a creative crayon box of colors exploded over his basketball jersey, adding to the work of art.

Carl's vision was blurry, but he could see the end. He got back on his feet and skated over, under and around the last few bursts of paint rainbows. Carl beamed with delight as he landed on the carpet and watched Joe finish. He ducked under a forest green colored cannon coming from his left, and did not see the burst of hot pink barreling towards him from straight ahead. It hit him square in the chest, knocking his feet out from under him. He rolled around on the ground to avoid the last few bursts of paint, and got to his feet on the semi-circle carpet. The paint had stopped shooting and they looked at each other. They were covered from head to toe in splatters of rainbow paint. They high-fived, sharing a gleaming grin.

"That was awesome!" they exclaimed.

~

"I don't understand what we're doing!" Kylie whined for the sixth time.

"I DON'T KNOW!" Eric shouted back.

They were in a classroom sized area with strange designs lining the walls. There was a single sheet of paper with random numbers organized in lines.

4 5 1 18

20 15 14 9

5 20 8

12 1 23 12

"Okay, so we know that we need a four word code to exit this room," Eric reasoned.

"We do?" Kylie questioned. "How do *you* know?"

"I -uh- might have tried to leave the room and a keypad with four word blanks appeared."

"Oh."

"Let's try having every number represent a letter," Eric suggested.

"Okay! A is 1!" Kylie shouted as if she discovered a solution to global warming.

"Duh," Eric replied as he scrawled in the letters.

Dear Toni Eth Lawl

"I know it!" Kylie shouted. "It's Dear Toni Eth Lawl!"

"*Oh really*? Why didn't *I* think of that!?" Eric replied sarcastically as he typed in the code. The door opened and they walked into the next mysterious task.

~

The answer from screen 8 appeared on Nysoum's data record.

"Dear Toni Eth Lawl? Ha!" Nysoum fell out of his chair laughing. "Anyone would know that's not right!" He chuckled once more, knowing that the blond quarrelers fell into his mouse trap.

~

"Go Adella, go!" Marisol supported her friend. They had known each other since kindergarten and were best friends ever since. They loved to do everything together, and the fieldhouse competition wasn't any different.

They were racing go-carts around the fieldhouse on a freshly tarred blacktop. They each had to complete three laps around the windy and hilly track. They each raced in a lane, cheering the other on as they progressed.

At the beginning of the second lap, Marisol hit an enormous rock. Her car slowed as a large amount of air leaked out of the tire with a whoosh. Adella hopped out of her cart (which was most likely against the rules) and she helped Marisol attach a spare tire onto the cart.

They drove around the enormous building and slowly but surely finished their three laps. Adella was sure that their time was atrocious, but at least they completed the three laps. But was it enough?

~

Noa Nysoum monitored all of his active screens. Adella and Marisol had finally finished the go-cart race. He recorded their time, but marked an x next to it, indicated that Adella had broken the rules when she exited her cart for a short while. He diverted his attention to screen 21.

Tim was incredible. How did he find his way into my fieldhouse? How did he know about the competition? All of the coded letters and various people involved were specifically meant to give the teams their fair chances of getting the info, but to keep outsiders from finding out. Clearly there was a flaw in that plan. Or more likely, one of the people he mistakenly trusted was not cautious enough.

And now, Tim was hopping on the lane numbers on the track like he'd done it before! 5 2 4 1 3 6. On the first try. Nysoum couldn't believe that kid. How did he even know that was what to do? Nysoum marked Tim's success and watched him leave the track.

Nysoum then searched his screens for little Rose. She was chewing on the pencil eraser on screen 19, with the logic puzzles. They were never her strong suit.

~

Where are John and Marta when I need them? Rose thought as she tore a hole in the paper by erasing too much. She grunted and launched her pencil across the room. When she went back over to pick it up, the tip was broken. She picked at it until a dull point reappeared. Rose reluctantly mosied back over to the logic puzzle to give it one last try.

There are 5 animals: A shark, an alligator, a gorilla, a condor, and a spider. Their names are B, Bo, Bob, Bobi, and Bobie. Their favorite colors are gray, black, brown, navy, and dark green. Using the clues below, find out the name and favorite color of every animal.

Clues:

1. The gorilla does not like brown, black, or navy.
2. Bo's favorite color is dark green.
3. The shark has a longer name than the alligator, but not the longest.
4. the condor's favorite color starts with B

5. the first letter of B's favorite color is the same as the first letter of the type of animal she is.
6. The alligator's name is a palindrome.
7. Bobie likes black, but the name with one less letter likes brown.

Rose read through the clues, but she didn't know what a palindrome was, and how could she figure out the shark's name that was longer than the alligator's, but she didn't know the alligator's name. Animals, colors, and names buzzed around in her head like bees. She was so utterly confused and desperate that she decided to randomly guess.

Shark - Bob - Gray

Alligator - B - Dark Green

Gorilla - Bo - Black

Condor - Bobi - Brown

Spider - Bobie - Navy

She slid her final answer paper into the slot and the door to the next room didn't unlock. Could she not continue because she randomly scribbled down answers? Was she stuck in this room forever until she answered this stupid puzzle correctly?

Rose hung her head and collapsed back into the chair. The more she thought about the confusing puzzle, the heavier her eyes grew. Her eyes drooped to a close, and just before she drifted off to sleep, Noa Nysoum's somehow familiar, booming voice returned on the loudspeaker.

"After your team finishes your current task, you will be escorted by one of my staff members back to the front entrance. Today's fieldhouse challenge is over. If you still wish to participate, come back tomorrow, same time, for more tasks."

After the message, Rose's door was still locked, and she couldn't pick the lock or break it down no matter how hard she tried. Within 5 minutes a fieldhouse staff member walked into her room and attached his key card back on the clip.

"Rose Hillary," he chanted in a robotic voice. "Please follow me to the exit."

~

Chapter 10

Marta and John left the building and breathed in the refreshing air. It was surprisingly light and the sun was gleaming. John forgot his watch at home but he guessed that was about 4 o'clock. The sun would start to set sooner, as fall and winter were approaching. It seemed as if they were in the fieldhouse for a long time, but John decided that so far he liked it. Marta walked over to where her bike was and saw Rose sitting quietly on the bench. She was waiting for them.

"Hi, Rose! How was your day of challenges?" Marta asked politely.

"Eh," Rose responded as she hopped off the bench and grabbed her scooter.

John took a quick glance at Marta and asked the unanswered question: *Is Rose still staying with us and for how long? Does she have a home? And where is it?*

"I know what you guys are thinking," Rose commented with a frown. My house is really far from here and if I go back, I will never see the light of day again. And I mean literally. I am not allowed to leave the tiny cottage. And that means I will never see you guys again and I will never complete another fieldhouse challenge. So I'm wondering if I could maybe stay with you guys for tomorrow's challenges, and I'll find someplace for the week. Please?"

"I think that will work," John said.

"Of course, Rose. We'll do it," Marta agreed. "You can stay with me tonight."

~

Once the stragglers had finally left the fieldhouse, Nysoum ordered his team to clean up the tasks and review the scores. They needed to be ready for the fresh start the next day.

~

Marta's phone buzzed. She went over to it to find Tim's goofy face on the front. Why would he be calling her? She picked up, but didn't say anything.

"Hello? Hey, Marta! How are you?" Tim asked kindly.

"Fine," she replied suspiciously.

"How were your challenges today? I bet they were all super easy for you. So, tell me all about it!"

Marta hung up. She wasn't going to give anything away to that snoopy cheater.

~

Tim couldn't help but laugh when Marta hung up on him. So like her. She wasn't dumb enough to give him any leads. But he knew someone who might.

~

Eric saw the number appear on his phone. He didn't recognize it, so he let it go to voicemail.

"Hi Eric! This is Tim Marloy calling. I'm in your grade at school and I saw you at the fieldhouse today. Congrats! So... call me back when you get a chance; I was wondering how you and your sis did on the challenges. Thanks, friend!" The call ended.

Huh. I don't really remember Tim, but he seems like a nice guy. Eric reasoned as he called back.

Tim picked up on the first ring. "Eric?"

"Uh, hi Tim."

"Eric! So glad to talk to you! How did you do during the competition today?"

"Great! We totally solved a secret code with numbers. It was Dear Toni Eth Lawl! What a tricky one, eh? I mean... quite easy actually. 1 was A, 2 was B, and so on. How about you, Tim?"

"Wow, Eric! Sounds like you did a great job!" Tim added with mock enthusiasm. "I have to go- my mom's calling for dinner. See you tomorrow!"

"Bye!" Eric hung up the phone feeling accomplished.

~

CHAPTER 11

Chapter 11

"We're late, come on Joe!" Carl screamed as he pushed Joe through the door.

"Welcome Carl and Joe. You are the first ones here," Noa Nysoum greeted.

They looked at each other in confusion. They had thought that it started at 7, and had arrived promptly at 7:15. Fortunately for them, the challenges didn't begin until 8.

Tim showed up next, promptly at 7:30.

"Welcome, Tim Marloy!"

Adella and Marisol came in and sat down next to Carl and Joe. They were followed by Marta, John, and Rose. Eric and Kylie came in last, but had plenty of time to spare.

"Rose Hillary, welcome! And uh, everyone else who seemed to walk in at the same time. You're all here, so let's begin. A staff member will come to escort you to the room you just ended in yesterday.

Marta and John gave a thumbs up to Rose, and allowed a young girl staff member named Alex to blindfold them. She then led them to their room.

John's muscles tensed as Alex took off the blindfold, and locked them in the tiny chamber. The room was divided into small sections with different doors to take and paths to travel. He was in one of the sections now, and was feeling a little claustrophobic. As his mind fogged up, he put the burden of choices on Marta.

She noticed tiny dots of color above each door. She didn't know what they meant, but decided to go with the bright green and it's positive connotation. John blindly followed Marta as she winded through doors and rooms to try and navigate the maze. After a while, he started to get a feeling that they were walking around in circles. He sat down and began to untie his shoe.

"You okay? What are you doing?" Marta asked, bewildered.

"I think we've been going around in circles. If we see my shoe here, then we know that the green doors go around in a circle," he reasoned as he slipped off his shoe. He put it in the middle of the room to be sure they wouldn't miss it.

"You're going to lose your shoe," she warned.

"Nah. With my memory, we've past this room about three times," he replied confidently.

Sure enough, they traveled through the green doors and eventually returned to the room with John's shoe.

"Go on, get it," Marta said, annoyed that he was right.

But John passed up his shoe.

"Now what are you doing?" she asked skeptically.

"We have to try the next color!" he grinned and chose the blue door.

Now Marta was following John through the blue path, until they reached the room with John's shoe once again.

"Purple," Marta suggested next.

Before long, they were back at the shoe.

"Red?" John tried.

They followed the path with the red symbol and John looked around for his shoe. They reached a room with a real fieldhouse door, not like the doorways with the colors from the maze.

"We made it!" John exclaimed, looking down at his foot. "And I'm shoeless."

Marta shook her head and laughed at her foolish brother. She couldn't help but say, "I told you so!" as she swung the door open to face the next task.

~

Carl and Joe were blindfolded and brought to the end of the room they had just completed. They had to chose where they were going next.

Joe grabbed Carl just before he opened a door.

“What?” Carl complained.

“That door’s unlucky. Let’s do this one,” Joe pointed to the one next to it.

“Whatever,” Carl replied easily.

They entered a door and were in a dark room with a very bright computer screen.

“Video game?” Joe asked hopefully. He slid the chair back to sit, but Carl plopped down in it.

“Thank you!” Carl smiled triumphantly and took control of the keyboard. His expression of excitement disappeared as he read the screen. He stood up and motioned for Joe to take a seat. “Here, bud. I’ll let you take the controls on this one.”

“Thanks, man! Joe beamed. He replaced Carl and read the first two words at the top of the screen: Trivia Quiz.

“Uggh! Gee, how *nice* of you,” Joe groaned.

Who was the 40th US President?

Joe Slobanite

"You aren't president!" Carl argued.

"Maybe I will be! We probably haven't had 40 yet, huh?"

Where is the capital city of Kiev?

On Earth

What is the chemical formula for rust?

Leaving a bike out in the rain

Name the too wrong things in this question.

1. Too should be two
2. ???

What is the cube root of 3375?

3375^(1/3)

Submit Answers

"Nice work, J Slob! Now let's get outta here!" Carl declared as the door swung open.

~

Adella and Marisol tossed off their blindfolds to find themselves in a room with tiled floor and roller skates sitting on a carpet. They had gone rollerskating together once, and it didn't turn out well. Adella had multiple bruises the next day, and Marisol broke her wrist.

"Dell? Do you know what we're supposed to do here?" Marisol asked nervously.

"Not sure. Let's take a walk down and see," Adella replied, trying to sound calm and comfort her friend's fear.

She stepped off the carpet and paint shot across the room, splattering Adella.

"AAAHH! My blouse!" Adella was appalled.

Marisol took a step and paint drenched her sandals. "Yuck!" she shouted, developing a concern other than breaking her wrist.

Adella ran, and with each step, more paint exploded above her, ruining her neatly curled hair and fashionable outfit.

"Eeeeeewww!" she shrieked with disdain. "My beautiful outfit is getting covered by paint!"

Marisol sprinted after her, trying to avoid the paint, but ended up running straight into it. Eventually they made it to the end of the hallway and regrouped.

"How do you get this stuff off?" Adella whined.

Marisol shrugged and tried to wipe her hands on her shorts. They got dirtier. "Uggh!"

"Come on, Marisol. It's not going to come off," Adella waddled over to the door.

Marisol nodded and slowly followed her best friend.

~

Once his blindfold was off, Eric confidently strode around the room. Tim had told him that he did a good job yesterday, and he was positive he would succeed with flying colors again today.

The only trouble was Kylie.

"A climbing wall? That's too hard!" Kylie complained.

Eric gazed around at the climbing wall with colorful handholds and footholds scattered around three sides of the room. He supposed they would climb it and see what else was involved in the task. He started to climb and dragged Kylie with him, but his legs quickly grew tired and he was out of breath in no time.

"There could be more to the challenge than just this. Let's conserve energy," Eric suggested as an excuse to take a break and hide his exhaustion.

"How about we go back down? My hands are so slippery and gross! We can find a door down there."

"Uh. Fine. What a whimp!" Eric muttered, yet he silently sighed in relief. He wasn't going to be able to go much further anyway.

~

Noa Nysoum watched as the siblings gave up and retreated. They safely avoided effort, and it cost them success. He recorded their task as a failure and considered their place in this competition. They were weak. They were not very smart. They were whiny. He had chosen them for a reason, but compared to the rest of these talented, unique kids, they seemed out of place. They didn't exactly fit the criteria he had in mind for his future team. They needed to be weeded out. But how? They had to decide to quit the task and leave the fieldhouse forever. But he could at least try to influence their decision.

But then something shocked him. He turned up the volume and leaned forward to watch screen 4.

"Kylie, are you ready? Let's go back up. We have to! Or we'll never get out..." Eric threatened.

"Okay, but you go first!" She shoved him forward.

Nysoum watched Eric slowly move up the wall. Kylie was below him, trying to pull on him to hoist herself up.

Pathetic execution, but surprising effort.

Still, they would have to be eliminated.

Nysoum called staff member Danny on the phone. “Lock down doors A,B, and D from room 4. A,B, and D!”

~

Chapter 12

Tim had flown through his first task and tried to recall which door Eric and Kylie went through yesterday. He picked one and closed it behind him. His memory never failed.

He found the coded paper and confirmed that Eric was correct. The message was indeed DEAR TONI ETH LAWL, but it didn't look quite right to Tim, and he knew it couldn't be that simple. He took each word and effortlessly unscrambled it. READ INTO THE WALL

Read into the wall? What did that mean? Tim examined the walls more closely and found strange hieroglyphs subtly carved in. He had to admit that he was more of a science and math guy, but he knew enough hieroglyphs to know that these were fake.

The first two symbols were a U and R, but the animals were poorly drawn figures, not glyphs. *U R What?* Tim thought. *That's it! You are what?!* Each animal must represent a team in the competition. He inspected the carvings more closely. There was a lion at the top, and 5 other animals below: A butterfly, a deer, a squirrel, a leopard, and a fox. Make that 6. There was an ant he didn't see before. There were seven symbols total and only six teams. Himself, Marta + John, Rose, the basketball players, the two kind girls, and Eric and his sister. Tim concluded that the lion on the top was Nysoum. He figured that he was trying to show his strength and superiority.

Tim began to eliminate the animals starting with the ant. He was too important to be a trivial ant. The butterfly and the squirrel didn't suit him either. They were too graceful and insignificant. He was not fast enough to be a leopard, and too cunning to be a deer. That left the deceitful fox.

Tim walked over to the door and the answer keypad appeared. There were four word blanks, so he typed in "I am the fox." The door clicked open, and Tim did not hold back a triumphant grin.

~

After ensuring that Eric and Kylie were forced to go through door 4C, Nysoum watched Tim. He intently surveyed the way he thought, and watched as he solved the code. The final answer streamed in, and Noa Nysoum smiled giddily. "Tim knows his place, as he rightfully should. And he knows my place, as he most *definitely* should.

He slid over to room 7 where Rose climbed into the go-cart. He watched her cluelessly sit there, baffled about what to do. Sympathy and a little bit of guilt washed over him, yet he was slightly amused. This kid didn't know how to drive a go-cart. She didn't know to press a pedal or even to steer. But even though she was at this slight disadvantage from poor parenting, he stood by and watched with a twisted smirk as she sped off out of control and passed the curve around the building.

~

Carl and Joe breathed massive amounts of fresh air. They were out of the trivia quiz, and were back in their comfort zone; they had found a track.

"Race ya!" Carl exclaimed.

"You're on!" Joe sneered.

The two athletes sped past the instructions for the task. They ran three miles and took a break.

"Didn't we pass it yet? I thought we ran enough!" Carl complained.

"Seriously, we're basketball prodigies, not track stars!" Joe agreed.

Carl found a water fountain that was right next to the task instructions. Something caught his eye about choosing different lanes and he called over Joe.

"Look! It says we need to find the right order of lanes to run in! That's why we didn't pass it yet!"

"But Carl, that will take forever! Running once in each lane is another mile and a half, and we don't know what the right order is!"

"You're right J Slob. We need to pick the order, run it, and be done."

"How 'bout 1 2 3 4 5 6? Seems easy enough!"

"Sure!"

And once again, they took off running.

~

Marta and John sat down at the desk and picked up the papers.

"Magic squares!" Marta beamed.

"Oh, joy," John rolled his eyes and relaxed in the chair until Marta finished the puzzles. He didn't want to admit it, but he was into them, too. He shouted out a few numbers before Marta could finish writing them down.

"Done!" She set down the pencil and slipped the pieces of paper into the slot. A good natured beep sounded and the door swung open.

"You know that feeling you get when you just took a math test and you immediately want to know your score? That's how I feel. We don't know how we did, or even why we're doing these tests!" John reflected.

"I don't know about you, John, but I thought that one was really fun! And besides, I checked our answers by adding up the columns, rows, and diagonals, just to make sure," Marta smiled at her twin brother, "and I was right!"

John stuck his tongue out at her and ran towards the next challenge.

~

Adella tossed her apple core into the trash can. A staff member had caught them in between challenges and gave her and Marisol sandwiches and apples. They were energized and ready to take on another challenge. They walked into a dark room with a staff member inside.

“Here, take this!” she said robotically as she handed them a pen and a notepad.

“Thanks!” Adella replied.

The staff member then flicked on a flashlight, waited a second, then turned it right back off. Next she switched it on and off in a flash.

“Dell, it’s morse code!” Marisol whispered, matching the dark mood of the room and flickering flashlight. “The longer ones are dashes, and the shorter ones are dots. You can right them down, and I’ll translate.”

“Okay,” Adella agreed softly. She immediately began scribbling dots and dashes onto the paper.

-• -•-- ••• --- ••- -- / •• ••• / - •••• • / ••- •-•• - •• -- •- - • /

-•-• •- •-• • - •- -•- • •-• / -• -• -•• /

•-•• • •- -•• • •-• / --- ••-• / ••-• •• • •-•• -•• •••• --- ••- ••• • !

•••• •• ••• / - • •- -- / •-- •• •-•• •-•• /

-•• • ••-• • •- - / •- •-•• •-•• !

“Wow, Adella! Great job! That was a lot,” Marisol praised. “Now, let’s see what I can remember.”

N?so?m is the ?ltimate caretaker and leader of fieldho?se! His team will defeat all!

“That must be a Y and the rest are Us,” Adella reasoned.

"Great! I think we're right!" The gleaming smile on Marisol's face melted into a frown," But what does it mean?" she asked in a terrified voice as she submitted their answer.

~

"You'll find out soon," Noa Nysoum cooed in a slippery voice as he confirmed their correct answer.

He then looked over at his many screens to notice Rose had successfully finished the go-cart race, but Tim was struggling on a challenge for the first time so far. He was trying to pass the art challenge, but ended up tearing a hole in his paper due to too much erasing. Nysoum didn't hold back his outburst of laughter. Tim might be a super smart genius, but he was *not* an artist. Nysoum decided to end the day of challenges on that comical note, not to mention that it would fire up Tim for having to end on a failure.

~

CHAPTER 13

Chapter 13

Marta and John made it outside. Marta looked for Rose but caught Tim's eye. He smiled and nodded his head upward to acknowledge her. She returned the kind gesture with a smile and a wave. She knew that the pressure of the competition was getting to him, but at least he was still his charming old self. As she was admiring his messy hair and his glasses sliding down his nose, Carl and Joe whizzed by on skates, knocking her over.

"Hey," John chased after them on his yellow skateboard. "Watch where you're going, guys! That was my sister!"

"JSlob, did you hear something?" Carl mocked.

"No, it must've been the wind," Joe replied with a smirk.

John fell behind and returned to Marta.

"Sorry about that," he mumbled.

"Don't worry about it," she responded. She watched Tim drive away in his sparkling car, while Adella and Marisol, and Eric and Kylie were leaving the fieldhouse. "Where's Rose?"

"I don't know, but she said she'd find a place for the week, right?"

"Yeah, but I wanted to make sure she'd be okay until next weekend." Marta looked worried.

"Look! There's her scooter. She left a note on it." John picked up the note card.

Found my place. I am good. Thanks for everything. See ya next weekend!

~Rose

"Oh, okay then. I guess she's alright." Marta buckled her helmet and followed John home.

~

Rose entered the fieldhouse through a door close to the go-cart race. Noa Nysoum was awfully suspicious. He was definitely holding back some secrets, and Rose felt obligated to uncover them. She was ready to break into the mysterious building and discover the truth.

The room she entered was light, and the challenge was still activated. The staff members must not have come through it yet. Rose hid in the shadows behind the screen and waited. She sat against the wall for ten minutes, readjusting her position to stretch out her legs. Suddenly, she heard a soft beep. Rose slid into the shadow further and watched as the staff member swiped his card again to lock the door behind him. He came over and sat down at the screen, inches away from Rose. She held her breath, afraid he would feel its warmth. He locked down the computer and looked for his key. It was now or never.

Rose used her agile footsteps to silently sneak directly behind the guard. Right as he unlocked the door, she took off her shoe and launched it across the room to the opposite wall. The guard jumped at the thud, and searched for the source of the sound.

"Who's there?" He demanded fearlessly.

But Rose had already swiped the key from the slot and slipped out.

She held onto the identification key card tightly. It was her ticket to any room in the fieldhouse. Or at least the ones that this guy could get into. But only one was important to her: The database archives. If there was top secret information about the stoic Noa Nysoum, she would find it there.

Checking behind her shoulder every minute for staff members, Rose used her key card to work her way through the maze of doors and rooms. Most of the tasks were already disabled, so she unlocked the door, walked straight through, and entered the next room. What she forgot to do was lock the doors behind her.

~

"Code yellow. This is code yellow. Many doors are unlocked!" a staff member named Alex reported.

"Follow the path of unlocked doors," Nysoum replied. "I will watch my screens."

"Craig to Noa Nysoum: My ID key card is missing!"

"Find it!"

"Yes sir," staff member Craig tried a door. Like Alex had said, it was unlocked. He passed through the room and picked one of three doors at the end of the hall. Locked. He tried another. Locked. The last one was unlocked, and he ran right through it, unable to lock it behind him.

"Scan fieldhouse!" Nysoum shouted to his control center.

Names and ages of his staff members appeared in different sections of the rooms. Then a siren sounded.

"Intruder, intruder! Rose Hillary! Age 9! Intruder!" The computerized robotic voice repeated the same alert.

"Rose?" Nysoum was bewildered. He did not expect the small 9 year old to break into his fieldhouse. He clicked on the message and the alert stopped, but the siren continued. The screen showed room 13 and Rose was slipping through the shadows. She unlocked another door and was headed in a diagonal path through the fieldhouse. In three more doors, she would be in the database archives.

"Lockdown all doors in room 13!" Noa Nysoum shouted.

But it was too late. She was already through to room 10. And now Craig couldn't chase after her because the doors to room 13 were locked.

"Unlock doors in room 13!" Craig ordered as he tried to get through.

"Unlock all doors to room 13!" Nysoum repeated angrily.

Craig burst through the doors and looked for the small red headed child. She was already in and out of room 13.

Nysoum watched Rose full on sprint to a door in room 10 and unlock it. She had one room left before the archives: Room 4, the climbing wall.

But that didn't even phase her. She quickly scaled up the wall and slipped through door 4D. She was in the database archives.

"Disable Craig's ID card!" Nysoum barked.

But Rose had already unlocked the exit as a precaution, and had used the card to get into the computer.

Search Files for "Noa Nysoum"

Loading...

Rose heard voices in the room she had just passed. She went to lock the door behind her, but the card was disabled. She went back to the computer, and a manilla folder appeared on the screen, stamped with a top secret seal.

Meant for the eyes of Noa Nysoum ONLY. All violators will be banished from fieldhouse and severely punished.

Rose didn't care. She was going to take the risk. She needed to know this information. The file opened at the click of a mouse, and she typed in an easily guessable password: NNysoum524136

Noa Nysoum

aNoNymous

Anonymous

That was irrelevant. She didn't care about the name. She scrolled down.

Noa Nysoum is a code name for the charismatic engineer from the outside woods of springville.

Springville? That was the town my father used to work at! No! It couldn't be. Rose thought as a tight knot of doubt and longing formed in her stomach.

She continued reading.

Roger Hillary, husband of Mary Verish, father of Rose Hillary, worked as an engineer in Springville. He left the family and town when the opportunity of leading a competition at the fieldhouse appeared. He thought it was best to leave six year old Rose behind, safe from the gravitational pull of the fieldhouse corporation. He knew that one day she might take part in the challenge of tasks, but the possibility of her progressing on to the next stage deeply concerned him, so he decided that young Rose would be safer with her mother.

Rose stopped reading. Noa Nysoum was her father? And he left her for this? But he had only tried to protect her from the thing after the competition. What would that be?

Rose's thoughts were interrupted by two guards, Mark and Danny, bursting into the room with tasers.

"Step away from the computer!" They ordered.

Rose put her hands up. She knew what she needed to know, and she was not in the mood to put up a fight.

~

CHAPTER 14

Chapter 14

It was a quiet and usual week for John and Marta, yet their main focus was on the fieldhouse competition. They went to school, absorbing a plethora of information like sponges. They wanted to learn as much as possible for the upcoming weekend of challenges.

Marta had suggested that she and John train physically after school to improve their scores on the athletic tasks. They went for runs, tried hurdles, climbed hills, and lifted weights. They did push ups, pull ups, and sit ups until their cores ached. She didn't know how much it'd help, but it was worth a try.

On Thursday evening, Marta went back on the fieldhouse website to make sure that the challenges were still happening at 8:00 on Saturday and Sunday. They were still scheduled as usual. But something was added on the site that hadn't been there before.

THE NEXT STEP BEYOND THE CHALLENGES!

Fieldhouse competitors- You think the challenges are difficult? They are just the beginning. Imagine taking part in an extremely perilous and exciting adventure to decide the fate of humanity? That only comes when you pass the tasks with unique success. Work hard during the challenges and we will see if you have what it takes.

Marta showed John the new online paragraph. He couldn't imagine what perilous adventure lied beyond the tasks, but it intrigued him. So far he enjoyed the problem solving challenges that tested his ability, and he was excited to take part in something more.

Knowing that there was more involved, John had an easier time in school on Friday. He was attentive in class and tried to actually understand the information that his teachers gave. And for the first time in his life, he was bored in study hall.

"What am I supposed to do?" he asked his friend Robby who was too engrossed in a video game on his phone to respond. "I'll be back." John decided to go to the gym and train more for the fieldhouse competition. He was ready to start up the challenges again.

On his way to the gym, John ran into Mr. Holland just outside of his classroom. He was the history teacher who had started it all.

"Hello John," Mr. Holland greeted.

"Hi Mr. Holland," John replied politely. "Oh, wait! Can I uh- ask you something?"

"What is it?" he asked as he closed and locked the door to his room.

"First I uh wanted to apologize for my behavior in class the other day." He thought it was best to start on a positive note. "And I also wanted to ask about the fieldhouse."

"Field house?" Mr. Holland looked confused.

"Yeah. Don't you remember the note you gave us? It led us straight to the fieldhouse." John quickly realized that Mr. Holland was not involved in the fieldhouse competition, so he stopped trying. But unfortunately, Mr. Holland would want to know why John brought up the subject.

"Why do you ask, John?"

Of course you had to ask.

"I just uh- wanted to tell you er... that I wrote my punishment essay there. One more question," John added quickly, before Mr. Holland would ask to see the essay. "Who is right about the names of the gods? Greeks or Romans?"

"Hmm, that's a good question. The Greeks came up with them first, but that doesn't mean they're right..."

"See ya Mr. Holland!" John scampered down the hall as his study hall period ended. He was thankful to escape Mr. Holland's history rambling, but he wanted to know: If Mr. Holland didn't put the envelopes there, who did?

~

CHAPTER 15

Chapter 15

The room was very dark, with no windows, no lights, no happiness. Bars lined the walls, serving as extra protection. The cell door was one of many in an enormous room, locked with a fingerprint sensor, voice recognition, and a five letter combination lock. The silence filled the tiny cell like thick smog.

Rose slowly opened her eyes and looked around the dark room. She hopped to her feet and slammed her fists into the barred walls.

“Let me out! I demand to see Roger Hillary this instant!” she shouted.

A staff member with the name Danny turned the corner with a flashlight and shone it directly on Rose’s face.

“Hey! Ow, stop it!” Rose shielded her eyes.

“Shut up! You are in a heap of trouble young miss. And do NOT mention that person. He has a new identity, and he will answer to it and ONLY it. Now, speaking of Mr. Noa Nysoum, you are to see him, now.” Danny entered the barred cell and locked Rose’s hands behind her back. “Walk,” he ordered.

Rose didn’t budge.

“Walk or I’ll force you to!” he repeated.

Rose refused to move an inch.

"NOW!" Danny shouted as he shoved Rose down the hall.

She didn't struggle against his force, but she didn't walk, either. She simply let him push her down the hall like a dummy until the finally reached another room.

Noa Nysoum himself opened the door. It was really him, Roger Hillary: the same old dad from three long years ago.

"Thank you Danny! You may leave," he announced.

Once Danny left, Noa Nysoum began. "Rose! Please understand. I left you for your protection! And yet I still knew that you'd figure it out and come here anyway. We could be a great team!"

Rose didn't know what to say. Her face was a combination of a death glare of hatred, and an exasperated look of longing and hope.

"But of course, dear Rose, there is one minor problem: You broke into fieldhouse and stuck your nose in our most important top secret files!! You are probably aware that the punishment is a strict banishment from fieldhouse. But we can't have you going around spilling secrets, can we? So that is where we use this!" Noa Nysoum pulled a sheet off of a giant machine with a red handcuffed seat, a black helmet, a giant touch screen computer, and a complicated keyboard.

Rose's sobs of disbelief turned into whimpers of fear, but she was not going to show her weakness to this man. Somehow, he sensed her fear anyway.

"Now Rose, don't be scared. Allow me to explain so you know precisely what I am doing to you. I have invented something fantastic! Such a terrific scientific breakthrough. I have discovered something I like to call the selective memory. We have another day of competition tomorrow, and we need you out of here by then. Don't want any competitors to run into you, do we?"

That was it. Rose needed to stall until tomorrow. Nysoum wouldn't do it when the others were around.

"Oh and I should mention that my touch screen and keyboard have my voice recognition and fingerprint sensors. So don't get any ideas," Nysoum added triumphantly.

"Whose voice does it recognize? Roger's or yours?" Rose snapped.

Nysoum was furious. "DO NOT MENTION HIM HERE!!"

"So you admit he's a different person!"

"NO! I mean yes? Wait, definitely not," Nysoum paused and thought about Rose's question. She was succeeding. He was truly perplexed, and time was ticking away.

And then he realized her plan.

"Don't think I don't know what you're doing! Stop wasting my precious time, you speck of dirt!" As he insulted her, he realized that his tone of mock kindness flew out the window. He tried to run after it.

"So now we will begin okay?" Nysoum maliciously rubbed his hands together before shoving her into the cold seat.

Rose instinctively fought back, but soon relented to a wave of deep darkness that enveloped her.

~

Danny tensed up and pressed his ear to the wall. He couldn't make out words, but most assuredly heard shouting. That contentious girl had started yet another argument, and his curiosity won out. He scanned his key card and unlocked the door. He cracked it open just enough to see the small girl get shoved into a metal chair. She screamed and fought back, but suddenly her limbs drooped and eyes closed.

"Noa Nysoum," Nysoum declared. The screen woke to a bright start.

Danny watched as various colored and sized dots appeared on the screen. Noa Nysoum slid his finger across the screen, as if searching for something. He gave up and moved on to the keyboard and each finger was scanned as it lightly tapped each letter. When he finished typing, a small brown dot appeared. He double tapped it and a trash can appeared on the screen. Noa Nysoum clicked it and the dot disappeared.

What did he just do? Danny thought.

Noa Nysoum returned to the keyboard and Danny watched his fingers more closely. He had typed out ROGER HILLARY and a bigger green dot appeared. He double clicked it and his finger hovered above the trash can. He decided against it and swiped out of the double click menu. He single tapped on the dot and similar dots appeared within the bigger green one. He held down his finger to select two of the dots. Danny squinted to read the labels.

Roger Hillary is Noa Nysoum

I saw Roger Hillary recently.

Then, without hesitation this time, Nysoum hit the trash can.

He quickly searched Noa Nysoum and nothing came up. He nodded his head with approval. He searched fieldhouse and again, nothing. Then he searched a bunch of names that Danny knew to be the other competitors: Kylie and Eric - Nothing. Adella and Marisol - Nothing. Carl and Joe - Nothing. But to his surprise, when he searched for Tim, a tiny blue bubble appeared. Nysoum clicked on it to see what was inside. He only found a short description of appearance and something about a robotics class. Nysoum wondered how Rose had found that out without being associated with fieldhouse. He deleted the blue dot and finished his thorough search with Marta and John. A big purple bubble appeared, filled with information about the twins. Nysoum wondered again how Rose found out all of this info without the connection of fieldhouse. He eliminated the entire bubble, and closed out of the computer.

Danny realized that he was going to be seen, and he hastily closed the door as Rose's body jolted to a start and her eyes snapped back open. Danny shook the image of the light flickering back into Rose's eyes out of his head and he ran out of the fieldhouse, reminding himself to stay on Nysoum's good side. But was Nysoum's side good?

~

CHAPTER 16

Chapter 16

"Did anyone see the news last night?" Tim's current events teacher asked.

The class collectively shook their heads and whispered comments.

"No one reads newspapers anymore!" someone remarked.

"I understand that Mr. Janston, thank you! And for the record, I do! But anyway, I think this is an issue that will intrigue many of you."

"Yeah right!" someone else snapped.

"Suit yourself Mr. Dill," Mr. Sullivan commented as he turned on the projector and found the video clip online. "But watch carefully because we will have a graded discussion after this!"

Tim grinned. The rest of the class groaned.

The newscast announcer began, "In the past week, many families in the town of Kollenburg have reported strange personality and behavioral changes in their children. Talented kids ranging from the young age of eight to the age of twenty have lost their smarts or their athleticism, and are reported missing at their schools and sporting events. Where are these kids going, and more importantly, where are these kids' talents?? And now we will move on the the hot topic of NFL Football."

Mr. Sullivan stopped the video and shut off the projector. "The student led discussion starts now," he announced.

"I wanted to hear about NFL Football!"

"Yeah, me too! Why'd ya turn it off?"

"The discussion is NOT about football gentlemen!"

"I'll start it then sir," Tim interjected. He was very interested by the topic.

"Thank you Mr. Marloy!" Mr. Sullivan sighed, relieved.

"What makes our town special? Why is this happening only in Kollenburg?" Tim asked.

"Great question Tim," Alice answered, "I think it might have something to do with the fact that our sports teams here are outstanding, and we have high quality education programs, don't we sir?" she asked looking over to Mr. Sullivan who nodded, determined not to contribute to the conversation that was meant to be *student* led.

"And so you think that our sports teams and schools attract bad guys to kidnap little kids?" someone snapped.

"No, not at all!" Tim added. "She means that because of our talents, someone has done something to those kids to make them... different. But who or how or why? Even I don't know."

~

Chapter 17

At the start of the challenges on Saturday morning, Nysoum greeted the competitors over the loudspeaker. "Hello everyone! This is Noa Nysoum with an update about Rose Hillary. She has decided to quit the competition and will no longer be involved in any fieldhouse events. On a separate note, a staff member will come to your team and escort you to the room you ended in last week. As *always*, best of luck!"

~

"Kyle and Erica?" The guard stuttered.

"Excuse me! Did he just say Kyle!!?"

"Haha! Come on *Kyle* let's follow him to our next challenge.

"Hm!" Kylie snorted in protest, but trailed behind.

The guard blindfolded them, and guided them down the hall. After a while he yanked the blindfolds off of their heads and left the room, leaving them to face the difficult task alone.

Right as the door closed behind the staff member, a siren sounded. Kylie collapsed to the ground in a trembling huddle of fear. Eric scoffed at her.

He walked a step forward and the black tile gave in. His foot fell through and was trapped in the ground. This was Kylie's turn to laugh. She got up off the ground and imitated Eric falling through the tile. But as she walked past an invisible laser sensor, a slight jolt of electricity surged through her body. All of her muscles tensed and released as she collapsed to the ground once again.

Eric watched his sister walk through the electric field. Her body jolted and suddenly slumped to the ground. His initial reaction was to laugh, but as she remained still in such an uncomfortable position on the floor, he decided that it was serious. He yanked his foot out of the fake tile and ran to help Kylie. He was oblivious to the fact that the electricity that hurt her was still activated, and was caught off guard when a jolt of electricity jerked his body out of control. His vision blacked out and he landed on Kylie.

The impact of something heavy landing on top of her woke Kylie to a start.

"Eew get off!!" She shouted at her older brother and tried to push him away.

He slowly came back to consciousness and saw that he was on top of his sister. He scooted away and warned her not to stand up again, the electricity was still flowing above them. And now, they were stuck underneath it, with no way to turn it off.

"I'm done!" Kylie whined. "This is stupid and dangerous! I won't do it anymore!" she shouted at her older brother.

He just nodded his head in agreement.

~

Noa Nysoum, who was watching Kylie and Eric with amusement, activated the loudspeaker.

"Is that your final decision? Do you wish to leave the fieldhouse competition once and for all?" He boomed.

"Please get us out of here!" Kylie sobbed.

"As you wish!" Nysoum declared a bit too happily. He disconnected the speaker to the room and contacted staff member Danny. He did well with difficult children.

~

"Carl, which path do you want to take?" Joe asked.

"I'll go on the low one. We'll put the taller person on the high path," Carl reasoned.

"Eat my dust!" Joe shouted.

"On your mark, get set, go!" Carl bursted through the tunnel as Joe sprinted across the suspension bridge. They raced each other through the obstacles, flying through like it was a piece of cake. Joe flew across the monkey bars, grabbing every fourth rung to propel him forward. Carl hopped over the hurdles like he was taking a layup, but he fell shortly behind Joe. He started to cross the river and lost sight of Joe as he flew down the enormous twisty slide. Carl refused to give up, and drove forward with each leap, trying to catch up to Joe. When he returned to the solid ground, Joe was climbing down a cargo net.

"I win!" Carl boasted.

"No you don't! I waited for you, loser!" Joe countered as he wiped the sweat from his face. "I watched from the bottom of the slide to see if I could still beat you if I waited ten seconds."

"Too bad, I still won!" Carl celebrated.

Joe grunted and followed Carl back inside the fieldhouse. Even if Carl won the race, they still demolished the course, and were ready to tear through another one.

~

Tim faced a triathlon, with running, biking, and swimming. He stretched a little before taking his mark on a three mile trail. He was supposed to run the first mile, and ride the bike for the second two.

Then at the end of the trail was a 100 yard long lake that he would swim across to the finish line.

When Tim was ready, he started to run, triggering the motion sensor that started the clock. His starting pace was too fast, and he exerted too much energy on the first half-mile. He slowed down, puffing, and finally reached the mile mark. He looked around for the bike. Where was it? He looked on both sides of the path and behind the trees. It was nowhere to be found. Tim decided to keep running, and see if it was just a little further on the path. No such luck. He heaved through the second mile and the bike was still missing. He was more than halfway through the race, and pushed himself to finish strong. When he finished the third mile, his eyes widened at the sight of the perpetual lake. He had forgotten about the swimming portion of the race, and was shocked at how long it seemed. Wasting no extra time, Tim jumped into the lake and started to flail his limbs to propel him forward. He swallowed water and started to drift off to one side. He was not an advanced swimmer, but he made it to the end. Tim got out of the water and found himself at another entrance to the fieldhouse. He found a towel on the door handle and dried himself off. Tim went inside, knowing that someone had sabotaged him, and he was not happy.

‿

John sat at the computer screen, furiously typing in answers to the trivia questions. This was more Marta's thing than his, but she had handed off the wheel to him. She stood against the wall in the corner, her eyes red and teary. She knew that Rose didn't quit; it wasn't like her. Something happened to her this week, and Marta felt responsible. Rose was like a little sister to her, and she couldn't help but feel like she had let her down. John finished up the quiz, but ran the answers past Marta before he submitted them. She might be too distraught to care right now, but John knew that this success was necessary for them to reach the next level.

"Hey Marta, are these right?" he asked.

She came over and corrected a few things. John smiled. As much as he hated when his sister proved him wrong, he was glad to see that she could still function properly. She hit submit and they left the room.

~

CHAPTER 18

Chapter 18

Rose woke up to find herself lying on the hard ground in her cottage with a throbbing headache. She couldn't remember anything. She tried to sit up, but more pain rushed to her head. Rose slowly walked over to the door and tried the handle. It was locked. As she sat back down, Rose slowly recalled her recent past. She had just experienced a terrible journey through the woods with lightning and thunder, and she had met someone in the village. But who was it and how did she end up back here? Where was her mother? Rose shook her head and decided to lay back down. She could hear the wood creaking underneath her mother's heavy footsteps, clunking down the steps. She heard the jangling of keys, the click of a door unlocking, and the shouting of an angry mother.

"Why did you leave me Rose Hillary? Where did you go?" her mother shouted.

Rose squinted her eyes and shook her head as if trying to remember. She said nothing.

"Answer me Rose!" Mary Verish repeated harshly.

"I- I don't know. I can't remember anything," Rose managed with a glare of confusion.

"Tell me the truth!!!" she angrily demanded.

Rose clenched her teeth. Something told her that it wasn't her fault that she couldn't remember anything, but she didn't understand it. Where had she gone after she left the town? Rose couldn't remember, but she knew someone who might.

Rose didn't bother arguing with her mother, so she lay down and pretended to fall asleep. When she heard a frustrated grunt and heavy footsteps climbing back up the steps, she jumped to her feet, punched through the window glass, and climbed out. Rose ran through the woods, feeling stronger than before. Energy and strength coursed through her body as she ran from tree to tree. Before long, Rose saw the town buildings in the distance. She continued to sprint full on into the face of the unknown. A bell chimed in her head as an old woman was walking down the sidewalk. She had talked to this woman before.

"Excuse me!" Rose shouted, chasing after the woman.

When she turned, the memories of talking to this woman flooded back to her.

"Rosalind! So great to see you, dear!"

Clearly, the woman's memory was not accurate either. "It's Rose," she corrected.

"Oh yes, I remember you!" The woman leaned closer as if she was about to reveal a secret. "What did the letter say?"

Rose looked up, puzzled. "What letter?"

"You know, the letter I gave you when you came here three weeks ago."

"What?"

A spark of curiosity flashed in the woman's eyes. "You mean, you can't remember?"

Rose nodded her head slightly.

"I know just what to do, Rosalina. Come with me."

"Rose," Rose corrected under her breath.

The woman brought Rose into her shop and she told Rose everything that she knew.

"So you're telling me that my dad left me to go somewhere for another job in engineering, but left a letter for me saying how to find him?"

The old woman nodded her head in agreement. "And I think, you had found him."

"What?" Rose's eyes grew big and her mouth gaped wide. She didn't know if she could possibly believe this crazy story. "But, why can't I remember?" Rose whispered in a small voice.

“Well I guess it all starts a long while back. I can’t remember much, as a matter of fact, my memories are very foggy from right around that time, but luckily I kept a journal with me. I have it here, see?” The woman held up a small journal filled with entries and started to read.

“October 4, 2015. Today Roger, some other woman and I just got recruited for a top secret government program working in a hidden underground facility. Its ultimate goal is to establish an equal utopia, where no person is more talented than another. This peaked our interest and we asked more about the program. They told us that we were chosen as ingenious scientists that would be suitable for the job of designing and creating a selective memory device that would be able to clear certain portions of one’s mind in order to neutralize their talents. We accepted, and today was the first day we traveled to the underground agency, and started to design the device.

“May 16, 2017. We did it! Today we finally accomplished our mission of designing the selective memory device for the government. We celebrated together as a team and the government thanked us for our hard work. Roger and I are satisfied with our accomplishments and are ready to leave the program, but Mallory doesn’t want to stop now. She thinks that in order to develop an even better utopia, we need to make a device that will add things that don’t really exist in someone’s mind. Roger and I disagree, and we think that Mallory’s idea is taking the government’s request a little too far. I don’t know what Roger and I will do about it.

"May 20, 2017. Roger and I decided to stop working for the government program because it was truly finished, and we are going to return to Springville tomorrow. I am going to open a small clothing shop in Springville and Roger plans to open some type of business. I think Mallory is going to continue to work on her own mission until she succeeds and I am scared.

"June 2, 2017. Today in Springville, Roger met a beautiful girl named Mary Verish. I knew it was love at first sight and I am very happy for him."

The woman looked up from her journal. "He eventually married Mary Verish, who is now your mother! Together, they raised you in that cottage a ways from here, all the way until you were six. But then Roger had to leave. I don't know where he went or why, but I have a feeling it has to do with our government program that seems like it was so long ago."

Rose was speechless. She had absolutely no idea if she should believe this outlandish story that this woman just told, but it sure seemed like it explained a lot about her father, and why she for some reason could not remember anything since her past visit to this town. She must have made it to her father! But what he must have done to her is even harder to believe.

~

CHAPTER 19

Chapter 19

"Danny, did you take care of Eric and Kylie yet?" Nysoum barked.

"Yes, sir, they're currently whining in the prison, waiting for you to- uh- do what you need to. It'd be best if you attended to them as soon as possible. Sir," he added.

"Of course. I shall go now. Will you monitor the screens? That's an order."

"Yes sir!" Danny excitedly sat down in Nysoum's large and comfortable chair. As Nysoum left the room, Danny watched the other competitors. He was one of Nysoum's head staff members, and he knew all of the secrets. Or at least he thought he did.

He knew Rose was a nosy and stubborn little girl who had meddled in serious business that was completely off limits. He knew that Noa Nysoum was formerly Roger Hillary and that he had left his family to develop some type of device and build the fieldhouse empire. He even had a pretty good hunch about what his unique device did. But what he did not know or understand, was how Nysoum could have possibly deprived his own daughter of the only memories she had of him, no matter how stubborn and blunt she was. After more thought, Danny realized why Nysoum did such a terrible thing; he was trying to save her from what was coming next.

~

"Marta?" John knocked on the door to her room.

"Yeah?"

John walked in and sat down on Marta's bed. He did this when he needed to talk to her for a while, usually about something serious. This worried her.

"We need to talk," he started uncomfortably.

Marta gulped. What was going on? John was starting to scare her.

"It's about Rose. I feel like Noa Nysoum isn't telling us the real truth, and I don't fully understand what happened, but I think I figured something out. Rose did something to make Nysoum really mad, and so she was banned from the fieldhouse. But he wasn't going to throw her out still knowing the secret location and missions of the fieldhouse. I bet he did something to- to make her forget-" John stopped because the look on Marta's face killed him. He had liked Rose, but to Marta, she was like a sister and a friend. He couldn't bear to see Marta so distraught, but he knew it had to be true. He patted her back supportingly and left the room.

~

"Welcome everyone. Today is the final day of challenges. I would like to announce that Kylie and Eric faced a rather excruciating challenge and realized that they did not have what it takes to make it through the competition. Similar to Rose, they will not participate in any more events at the fieldhouse and they are back to living their old lives. Please don't be alarmed if they don't remember you, and DO NOT TALK ABOUT THE FIELDHOUSE WITH THEM OR ANYONE ELSE, EVER!! Thank you!" Nysoum chose his words carefully and spoke with persuasive charm.

Marta shot a look towards John. He was right. Nysoum was truly and gruesomely evil. But the more sickening thought was that if they quit now, they would suffer the same fate.

~

Tim wiped his glasses and flipped his hair before he tried to continue the taxing task. He was sitting at an ancient computer that had no volume, and half of the keys on the keyboard were broken. And yet, he was asked to hack into a system and create an internal virus within the site. Tim's eyes were burning from the intense glare emanating from the screen, and his hands were aching from the awkward position on the keys. Most of all, his brain was erupting with frustration and impatience. The computer froze multiple times, and took forever to process any of the information Tim tried to thrust at it. Tim was losing and he didn't know what to do about it. Technology was his strong suit! Nysoum would be thoroughly disappointed in him if he failed this task, so he returned to the drawing board, where he came up with plan B.

Tim obliterated the keyboard. Each key flew off into space as he continued to smash until he reached the circuit board. Tim then carefully took apart the monitor and rebuilt the entire system, creating a faster processor, and a projected light keyboard, enabling him to easily hack into the complex system, passing the challenge.

~

Carl and Joe stood in a room that simulated a volcano. The ground was crumbling beneath their feet, and red hot lava spurted across the sky. The ground shook and split into two halves, creating large chasms of burning lava between them. The rocks beneath Carl crackled and sank in the burning flames. He leaped to another rock, but the scalding lava enveloped his ankle. He was separated from Joe, but they both knew what they had to do. The exit door was inside of the volcano, and the only possible way to get in was to climb into it and trudge through the flames. Joe looked around him. There was lava everywhere, bursting through the crumbling ground, dripping down the scorching pyramid. The flames were attacking him, so he decided that the best form of defense was offense. He hauled a chunk of hard ground over his head and set it on fire by using it as a shield to block the flames. He then used it as a weapon and he launched it into the heart of the volcano. It erupted as it came into contact with the bubbling surface, and eroded a portion of the volcano wall. Joe realized that he could tear down the volcano to access the door instead of climbing inside. He continued to launch chunks of flaming ground back at the volcano, making notable progress.

Carl dodged the extra splashes of lava, also noticing the collapsing volcano. As the walls of the grumbling volcano depleted, Carl jumped over, under, and around bursts of lava to reach the center, where the door was located. He vaulted over the remaining wall, bracing himself for a burning pain. But it never came. He landed softly inside a protected capsule preventing flames from destroying the door. He tried to shout to Joe that he was alright, and it was clear to come inside, but instead he saw him try to get in by running headstrong into a wall of fire. His body blistered with burnt dead skin and his clothes combusted into flames. Joe tried to keep running, but only slammed against the invisible capsule wall and collapsed to the ground right before Carl's eyes.

~

Adella stood in the spacious room and considered her few options. Two things needed to be done simultaneously. Most people would say she had an easy solution, because one person would take one job, the other on the second. The problem was, Adella and Marisol viewed themselves as one team, not two people. They wanted to do everything together, and they always had. But now, Nysoum was forcing them to split up and work separately. There were two curtains, one with Marisol's name written on it, and the other with hers.

"I guess I'll see you in a minute," Marisol quaverred nervously and stepped through the curtain with her name on it.

"Okay," Adella responded to the empty air hovering around a closed curtain. She drew back her curtain and walked through to find piles of various colors and types of clothing material. Seeing the clothes awakened a bright spirit of hope inside of her. This was one thing she knew well.

Adella noticed a small bowl of water, a candle, and a scroll of paper sitting on a table in the corner of the area. She walked over and easily read the flowing lines of cursive, instructing her to find the piece of clothing material that was both fire and water resistant. *Does such a thing even ex-*

ist? I sure haven't heard of anything like it! Adella thought. *But anything is possible, even pink and red.* She shuddered at the idea of the two clashing colors within the sea of aquamarines and periwinkles. *I'll find the right material, and I'm sure it will have the perfect color scheme!*

~

Marisol's heart skipped a few beats and immediately started racing. There was someone sitting in the room! She was initially startled, but then intrigued by the girl sitting there. She was pretty with chestnut brown hair and deep brown eyes, wearing a staff member badge with the name Erin written on it. But when she started to talk, Marisol was shocked once again. The foreign words flew out of her mouth sounding like nothing but gibberish. Even though Marisol didn't understand a word Erin was saying, she knew that she would have to translate it, and most likely answer the question or perform the command. Marisol used what she knew from taking French in school, and tried to match the roots of the words to what she knew in English. She came up with something like "The friend of you is in a gravy dish."

~

Adella tried dipping the clothes into the bowl of water. If they absorbed it and became damp, she would throw them into the trash bucket. If they resisted the water, she threw them into a pile on the ground. She sorted out all of the clothes, finding sixteen materials that were water resistant. *Now I test for combustibility* she thought logically. She grabbed the first material from the sixteen that were water resistant, and held a corner into the flame of the burning candle. As expected, it caught on fire, the licking flames dancing further toward Adella's hand. She dropped it on the ground and tried stamping it out. Eventually, the flames subdued. Hesitantly, Adella chose another material and tested it in the small flame of the candle. It too, caught fire and burned to crisp ashes. She was starting to get very uneasy. What if she caught on fire?

~

Erin repeated the same message of gibberish over and over again that Marisol translated to something like "The friend of you is in a gravy dish." She knew that couldn't be right. "The friend of you" might just be "your friend", referring to Adella, and gravy dish must mean something else. She thought of things similar to "gravy dish" like groovy wish or grainy fish, but none of those sounded right. Why would Erin be telling her that Adella was in something, anyway. The only thing that mattered to Marisol was that Adella wasn't in trouble, and Marisol had a pretty good feeling that she was okay. Then it hit her like a box of building blocks. *Adella isn't in a gravy dish; she is in grave danger! And she needs my help!* "Thank you!" Marisol shouted to Erin as she spun on her heel and back out through the curtain. Without hesitation, Marisol plunged through Adella's curtain. Whether she was supposed to be in there or not, she didn't care. She just wanted to help Adella.

When she walked in, everything was engulfed in flames, and Adella was rolling on the ground, trying to put out the malicious flames dancing through her body. Marisol panicked. She could smell the thick smoke and her eyes were starting to water. Adella extinguished the flames on her outfit and shakily pointed to her pile of waterproof materials. There were only two left, and one of them had to be fireproof. Marisol followed her finger and threw one of the clothes into the burning flames. It didn't catch fire, and the flames actually subdued, because they could no longer get enough oxygen.

"Quick Adella! Grab all of the ocean blue colored fabrics like this!" Marisol shouted and continued to use it to put out the spreading fire. Adella obeyed and before no time, the fire was gone, and a secret closet door opened. They regrouped and walked through to the next challenge.

But it never came.

They walked through the halls and ended up back in the fieldhouse lobby, where they found Erin again.

"Hey, girls! You did an amazing job!" Erin praised. She shocked Marisol for the third time when she spoke English again. "The challenges are over now, so just relax until Nysoum gets here."

But at that moment, relaxing was one of the last things Adella and Marisol could think of doing.

~

Chapter 20

"Be careful, now Rosabelle! I hope you know where you're going!!"

Rose scowled and muttered, "Rose," as she thanked the woman and left the town. She was starting to vaguely remember coming this way before, validating the woman's unfathomable story. Rose still couldn't understand how her father could have done such a thing to her. He was funny, charismatic, and kind, not evil and selfish. She believed that she could restore her father's true character if she returned to him saying that his invention had failed and that she was forgiving him with open arms by offering a second chance. The only problem was, his terrifying invention actually worked, and she could not remember anything about this matter. The only things she knew were from the old woman, and Rose didn't know if she could depend on someone who couldn't remember a simple name like "Rose."

In some miraculous way, Rose reached the clearing at the woods by the fieldhouse. It matched the directions that the woman gave, but Rose still didn't recall having been there at all. She saw two kids older than her, racing in little cars around a track that surrounded the gigantic building. One was a girl with long brown hair flowing with the wind, and the other was a boy with messy brown hair. From a distance at least, they looked pretty similar, and she thought that they could be related. They turned a corner and were no longer visible. Rose waited until she could see them in the distance on the other side of the track.

Clearly, they saw her too, and their faces lit up at the sight of her. She wondered why, because she surely had never seen them before. They immediately stopped their little cars and ran over to her location on the edge of the woods.

"Rose! Rose! You're back!! We knew it didn't work. You're too tough and smart for his old tricks!" The brown haired boy shouted.

She slowly shook her head. He was very wrong. She had absolutely no idea who either of these people were, but clearly, they thought they were her best friends.

The girl looked crushed. "You mean, you don't remember us?" she asked in a small, dreading voice.

Rose shook her head once again. "I don't know who you are, who someone named "Noa Nysoum" is, or even who I am, really. I might be in some crazy dream, but even if I am, tell me what really happened as best as you can so that I can tell a big story about it."

"Alright," the boy started, taking on the task. "You are Rose Hillary, and you found us coming home from school. Marta saw your letter, and-"

"What letter?" Rose asked.

"It was a coded letter inviting you to this fieldhouse competition," the girl named Marta added.

The boy said his name was John, and he recapped all of the events up until Nysoum wiped her memory. It was a miraculous and skeptical story, but Rose believed every word.

~

Danny watched the outdoor go-cart screen as a flashing red light blared and an alarm sounded. Fieldhouse's first intruder was a short girl with bright red hair that he knew to be none other than Rose Hillary. How did she get here? Did Nysoum's machine not work? But Danny knew one thing for sure, and that was that Nysoum would not be happy about it.

~

Today was the last day of challenges. Nysoum needed to stream in the final data, and calculate the final results. He had an idea of who he thought was ready to proceed, but the data would tell him everything. But instead of working with the numbers in his tech room, he was wiping Kylie's mind. He had just done Eric's, which had gone well. Kylie was more difficult, because her brain was structured very differently. She had a lot less information, and it was not very organized. Nysoum groped around for every last detail about the fieldhouse and everything in it. Suddenly, an alarm sounded and his machine automatically shut down.

"Code red!" Danny shouted to Nysoum over the loudspeaker. "We have an intruder. Rose Hillary has somehow returned!"

"WHAT???" Nysoum was furious. How had Rose come back?? Was the machine he had built for the government so long ago a failure? "Where is she?" he demanded.

"Out in the go-cart track with the twins. What should we do?" Danny asked, instinctively rubbing his hands together.

Nysoum thought about everything he needed to do. If anyone, he could trust Danny to do this job. "You know the drill. Go get 'em!" Nysoum ordered as he shut down the alarm and reentered into his machine. He refused to admit that his confidence was majorly busted after Rose's return. Did she remember everything? And even worse, did she know what he had done to her? With these doubts swimming around in his brain, Nysoum finished wiping Kylie's mind, just in case his machine actually did work.

When he finished, he brought the two back to the caged room, where one of his staff members could bring them back to their home. Someone else could handle that job. He and Danny had been a little busy recently.

~

Danny burst out of the doors to the go-cart track and pointed his stun gun at Rose. Marta leaped in front of her to protect her, and John in front of her. *How cute!* Danny sarcastically thought. He inched towards them, hoping he wouldn't have to hurt them, but he would if he needed to.

"Don't come any closer!" John shouted, frightened of what Nysoum would do to them if they were defenseless. (Which, they pretty much were, but at least they were conscious.)

Danny didn't stop walking and John kicked the gun out of his hand when he got close enough. Rose snuck around behind him and picked it up. She pointed it at Danny, who laughed. To him, a little girl holding his stun gun was a funny picture. But he didn't realize how sharp of a shooter she really was. The smug smile was frozen on Danny's face as he slumped to the ground.

Marta held the guard's feet and John pulled his arms. They dragged him to the front door where they knew Nysoum had extra high tech security cameras, and laid him limp on the doorstep.

Rose drew four words in the dirt, creating a caption that perfectly depicted their triumph. Don't mess with us!

‿

Chapter 21

Adella looked to Marisol with hope and anticipation. They had made it through the challenges, even the messy ones, and were now waiting in the fieldhouse lobby with the other remaining competitors: Carl and Tim. From Carl's stories, they all learned that Joe was still in the competition too, he had just gotten badly burned in their final challenge, and was getting medical help from one of the staff members.

Rose had been gone before yesterday, and Eric and Kylie were gone this morning. But where were the twins? Adella knew she had seen them this morning. Just then, two staff members named Alex and Mark walked in. A beaming Carl followed them, though his skin was covered in red blisters.

"I am here to announce who has advanced to the next level. All of you have different strengths and weaknesses, which are hard to compare. You will all advance to the next round, where you will be further tested and challenged. Meet here next Saturday at 8, and we will explain the next level. Congratulations," Alex said cheerfully and walked away with Mark. Erin shortly realized that she was the only staff member still in the room, so she said goodbye to Adella and Marisol on her way out.

~

Everyone made it? That seemed awfully sketchy to Tim. And, he couldn't help worrying about Marta. What had happened to her? Tim decided to call her. No answer. He left a short message though truly wanting to have a long, pleasant conversation face to face. He decided that tomorrow, he would make the longer trip from school to pass the middle school on his way home. He grinned at the thought of a leisurely stroll and conversation as he would escort Marta home from school. But then he remembered about John. He would ruin everything simply by being there.

By Sunday night, Tim had a complicated plan all worked out. He would use a bug to leave a note in John's backpack that was "from his best bud Robby" that him to meet him at the park right after school. John would then go to the park after school, leaving Marta available to walk home with Tim.

On Monday morning, Tim discovered that he didn't need to have to worry about getting rid of John; he wasn't in school today. But Marta wasn't either.

During the rest of the week, Tim focused on his school work, but didn't let that distract him from the competition. He worked on his bugs and designed more robots, thinking that he could somehow hack into Nysoum's security system to find Marta. On Friday evening, Tim packed his technology into his black truck, and drove to the fieldhouse. He was hiding in the woods, but the fieldhouse was in sight.

First, Tim pulled out his caterpillar. It slowly crawled up the path and onto the dirt driveway. A red laser from a security camera pointed at it, and it combusted into flames. Before Tim did anything else, he would have to shut down the security. Or at least the front entrance part of it. He used his laptop and got into the fieldhouse website. He ferociously pounded out code on his keyboard, but his first attempt was blocked by a complex level of defense and protection. Tim tried again, this time with a little more results. He was able to turn on a light in one of the rooms. It didn't seem like much, but it was a start. He turned on the light and continued tapping out code.

~

"Who's there?" John shouted.

No one answered.

"Did you guys see that light turn on?" he asked.

"Yeah, but I don't hear anyone," Marta replied.

"It's a ghost!" Rose suggested. "Where are you, Nysoum? You coward!"

Rose's high pitched but confident voice echoed through the halls.

Nysoum heard their conversation and had also noticed that the light had turned on. He was in the middle of delegating roles for Saturday, and soon realized that Rose, Marta, and John were needed for the team's success. He added them to the list of team members and gave them their positions. They would wait in the prisoned hallway until Saturday as a punishment, but then he would welcome them back to the team. As much as he thought they needed punished, they were needed to fight Malevita.

~

Tim didn't want to, but he was forced to give up. Nysoum's security was too strong for him to hack into, and it was getting late. He would arrive early tomorrow morning and confront Nysoum about Marta.

~

Chapter 22

When Tim arrived at the fieldhouse, Marta was sitting on the ground with John and Rose, talking to the staff member named Mark. Tim joined them, somehow plopping himself down right in between Marta and Mark.

“Marta! I was so worried. Where were you after the challenges last Sunday?”

“We-”

“They were with me,” a deep voice declared as Noa Nysoum, the mysterious man himself, entered the room. “And I was amused by your tricks last night.”

Tim turned red. He was meeting Noa Nysoum in person for the first time, and Nysoum knew that Tim had hacked into his system.

“Sir! It’s- an honor to finally meet you in person!” Tim declared as a last minute attempt to switch the subject.

“Yes, well, we have a lot to discuss today.”

Adella and Marisol walked in and gasped. They were shocked by Noa Nysoum’s real physical presence. They shrank against the wall to sit with the staff member, Erin. Carl and Joe ran in, panting. Clearly, they had run all the way here.

"Alright. First I would like to congratulate you for making it this far in the challenges. They have been difficult, but let me assure you, that they are preschool compared to this next mission. There is someone evil, who is trying to take over everyone's minds. She uses a brain altering device to wipe away all your memories, knowledge, and talents. Then she replaces it with terrible things, without your noticing. This evil woman is Malevita. You are all needed with your unique, individual talents, and team assets, in order to defeat her mind distorting empire."

Noa Nysoum paused to let the information sink in, and the children absorbed it like sponges.

That was why Nysoum created the memory machine! He was only trying to reverse what Malevita did. Maybe he wasn't so bad after all. Marta thought.

Staff member Danny had just walked in with an ipad, and everyone turned towards him. Alex followed him in.

"Ah, Danny, just in time. Please proceed," Nysoum interjected.

Danny cleared his throat and started to read a list of names and positions: The starting line up.

"Tim: Education and Technology Advancement Wizard.

Carl: Runner.

Joe: Runner and Weapons Master.

Marisol: Communications and Teamwork Leader.

Adella: Advertising and Style Manager.

Rose: Runner.

Marta: Code and Puzzles Creator/Interpreter.

John: Quick Thinking/Decision Maker and Runner."

"Thank you, Danny. I have a letter for each of you that describes your roles and duties. Please read it and understand it, for we will begin training immediately. Welcome to the team!" Nysoum declared as he handed out the papers.

Marta looked at the paper given to her. It was filled with random letters and she immediately recognized that it was a cryptogram. She realized that Nysoum had already begun training them, and she knew this task was meant especially to test her. If she was to prove her worth as the code and puzzles creator/interpreter, she would have to decode this thing, and fast.

John was thinking along the same lines, because his paper was specialized for his new job, too; it was a map. He had to read the choices at each intersection and navigate his way to the end. When he completed the path, he read a paragraph that perfectly explained his job as the decision maker. But he wasn't sure if he liked it. A five ton weight of pressure was just dropped on his shoulders.

Joe nudged Carl. "Hah," he whispered, "I'm weapons master and your just a plain old runner!" He grinned like a little boy getting a balloon, and looked at his paper with pictures of various weapons.

Carl shot him a look and stuck out his tongue. He returned to his paper, which had one word on it: Run. And so he did. Carl took off running around the room and "accidentally" knocked Joe over. Nysoum observed his reaction, and compared it to Rose, who was also a runner. She read the word, tossed the paper on the ground and sat down with a defying glare. Marisol had morse code on her paper, and Adella had artistic images that she had to interpret. Tim's paper was written in computer code. Everyone had at least some idea of what to do for their job, except Rose.

Staff member Alex observed this and confronted Nysoum with a suggestion. He nodded his head and started to speak, "Rose, I am adjusting your role. You are now a gunner."

"A gunner?" Rose stood up with anticipation.

"Yes, but I'm not going to bother giving you another paper. Your job is to go and investigate Malevita's headquarters, and try to figure things out. You will break down as much as you can, with your new weapon that Tim and Joe will make for you. Do not get caught! You are our secret spy. Understood?"

"Yes, sir!" Rose agreed, hopping up and down.

"Good. By now, the rest of you should understand your roles, too. Throughout the challenges, I was testing you for spots on the team, and training you for these specific roles. You each have a command on your paper. You have two days, today and tomorrow, to complete it. Starting Monday, we begin our mission to Malevita's evil empire, so get your job done and done perfectly! Oh, and by the way, our staff members are also part of the team.

They have their own roles, and will *not* help you with yours. Trust *yourself* to get your job done. Meet Erin, Mark, Alex and Danny," Noa Nysoum announced.

"Where's Craig?" Alex inquired.

"Gone," Noa Nysoum responded easily.

~

Chapter 23

Alex was the computer genius at fieldhouse who had set up the powerful firewalls that Tim couldn't penetrate. She brought him to the tech room where they would work together to try and hack into Malevita's system.

Adella's task was to design and create uniforms for everyone on the fieldhouse team. She was overwhelmed with excitement. She started with a sketch of a design and perfected it until she knew they would be stylish spies. Then she referred back to her paper to find out that she also had to make the suits flexible, water tolerant, and fire resistant. Adella knew that a fire resistant material existed because of her challenge, but she didn't know what that material was. She conducted some research and couldn't find anything. She decided to go speak with Joe, the weapons master, who had to have a fire resistant material or coat of some sort.

Of course, he didn't. Joe sat in one of Nysoum's rooms lined with gadgets and weapons of all sorts. He fooled around with them, just as Nysoum had said. He was "testing them out." Adella rolled her eyes and concluded that she would have to design the material herself. She grabbed a small flame launcher and left the room.

"Hey, you girl, come back here!" Joe shouted.

Wow, he doesn't even know my name. Adella thought. But being the considerate and kind person she was, she returned to Joe.

She took the time to acknowledge his height and features as she stepped in the doorway and introduced herself. "Hi Joe, I'm Adella. It's nice to meet you! Is it okay with you if I borrow this flame launcher to design a fire proof material for our uniforms?"

"Hm," Joe considered her request without looking up from his gadget. "If you put our last names on the back like basketball jerseys."

Adella considered his request. Nysoum would kill her if she designed suits with everyone's last names on the back. That would reveal personal info to the enemy. "Sorry Joe I don't think Nysoum will see that as acceptable," she suggested.

"Code names, then?" Joe asked hopefully.

"Uh- I'll try my best," she conceded.

"Alright. Thanks, Della," Joe stared as she smiled charmingly and left the room.

Adella returned to the room where Marisol was creating light key chain sized flashlights for everyone to communicate through morse code. She helped Tim to make bluetooth ear pieces for their main communication, but when they needed to be silent, morse code was a good second option.

"Marisol, how are you doing? I like the flashlights."

"Thanks, Dell! I'm good. How about you?"

"I'm trying to design fire proof material for our uniforms, and the only way I could get Joe to give me the necessary materials was to agree to put code names on the back of them. Do you think Nysoum will agree to that?"

"I don't know..." Marisol replied. "Why don't you ask John? He's the decision maker, right?"

Adella took the list of code names to John, who vetoed the idea.

"It's a cool idea, but I don't think Nysoum will agree. And plus, he won't be able to keep track of us. And anyway, I pretty much just learned your name, Marisol!"

Adella looked at him with a smirk. She didn't mind being called Marisol (since they were best friends) but it was amusing to think that she and John had been working together for a while now and he still hadn't learned her name.

"Or is it Erin...? I'm only joking! I know you're Adella. But actually, I think I have to say no on the code names."

~

Marta had to create an entire new code and code ring for them to use. She did some research about historical code rings that were successful, and designed a complicated system of dropping and recovering invisible ink coded messages in certain spots in and around the fieldhouse, and would soon make one for Malevita's headquarters, but she needed the layout from Tim or the runners if he couldn't hack into the system. But she had full confidence that he could.

John was instructed to supervise the events until Monday, when he would lead the group of runners to Malevita's headquarters. He mostly hung out with Marta, but helped Joe design and deal out weapons for Rose, Carl, Joe, and himself. He was excited to lead the expedition of spies into the unknown enemy territory, but he was nervous about his new position as the decision maker. Something was telling him that he would have to make a decision that would make or break the team, yet Marta assured him that Nysoum would make most of the important decisions.

"He's such a maniac control freak that he won't be able to go five minutes without dominating the universe!" she laughed, but was really telling the truth.

"That may be true, but he's going to have to make more decisions than he thinks." Nysoum happened to be walking by as Marta teased him. She turned red with embarrassment and John tried to cover up her mistake with another one of his infamous charming jokes that usually end up becoming his own downfall. The last time he tried to joke about something serious, he ended up stuck in before school detention for a week.

"Don't worry, Nysoum, when Malevita gets ya, you won't even remember that Marta threw you in the toaster for a little too long!"

"Indeed, Mr. John. But let me advise you, if my memory is and very well may be distorted, I am going to ask you to take the lead." And with that, Nysoum disappeared to go check in with the others.

John turned a ghostly color. "How did I suddenly get all of this responsibility?"

~

Chapter 24

"Tim to Rose: Alex and I just hacked into the security cameras. We will check your surroundings as you investigate. As of now, the coast is clear. Be safe and I will stand watch."

"Right," Rose responded, focusing on her task. She was sitting on a skinny tree branch, suspended 30 ft. in the air. Despite the height, Rose wasn't phased. She felt comfortable and excited as the adrenaline rushed through her coursing body, anticipating an eventful attack. She had been very experienced with heights ever since she was climbing trees with her father at the age of four.

She used her spy glasses to zoom in closer to the empire, where she saw tall guards patrolling on segways. For a psycho technology mastermind, the amount of protection around the building didn't seem too extensive. But then she switched her spy lense to sense the invisible booby traps, and the scene lit up like a Christmas tree.

"Rose to Tim: There is a force field, an electric fence, multiple laser beams, voice and physical appearance recognition, and security cameras," she reported, trying not to sound too intimidated by the extreme security.

"Don't worry, I already said we're in control of the cameras," Tim replied nonchalantly.

"Yeah, that's *great.* One thing out of a million can be scratched off our list!" Rose sarcastically snapped, feeling less confident about her job as a gunner. She had to admit, she was a bit nervous about breaking into an enormous building that she had no idea what lurked inside. Then again, she easily snuck through Nysoum's fieldhouse to find his computer information database, and regretted her actions as she recalled poor Craig's misfortune. She put it out of her mind, because now he was ignorant to it all. And sometimes, she reflected, ignorance was bliss.

"Alright miss demanding, we're on it. Stand by," Alex reported.

~

Mark and Joe were going to look at things from a different view. They boarded a small helicopter and Mark expertly manipulated it up and away from the mysterious woods surrounding the fieldhouse. Joe tried to imagine what it would be like to control the heavy chunk of metal. He knew that if it were him sitting in that pilot's seat, his face would be gleaming, plastered with a giddy childish grin. He looked over at Mark, who was impassive. His face was impossible to read, and Joe couldn't tell if he enjoyed flying the copter or not. But he knew one thing for sure, and that was that Mark took his job very seriously, and flying a helicopter was definitely one of his prowesses.

"Hey Mark!" Joe shouted playfully. "How long have you been flying copters like this one?"

"I'd say about five years," he replied easily, with about as much emotion as a stone wall. He waited for a follow up question.

"And how did you find the fieldhouse?"

He paused for a while as if trying to decide if he was going to say something or not. "Well, I once participated in the challenge competition just like you kids, not too long ago," he mumbled and his voice trailed off.

Joe's gaze once again moved from the passing clouds back to Mark. "And?" he asked hopefully.

"I wasn't too good at the puzzle and code sort of challenges, but I dominated the active ones. Kinda like you and your buddy Carl," Mark added. "I had a-" He stopped again.

"What?"

"I had a teammate named Meg. She was one of my biggest rivals from sports games, and well, she was really smart, too. We joined forces for the competition, and we totally rocked the obstacle courses. Nysoum said we were the fastest ones our year, and we were so proud. And by the way, no one beat our record!! Did you guys ever get to the obstacle course?"

"Yeah we did," Joe responded shamefully. He was disappointed that he didn't beat Mark's record.

"But uh, she didn't make it through to the next step."

"What happened to her?"

"She's- she's on the other side now."

Before Joe could think of something funny to lighten the mood, something appeared on their radar. Joe stole a quick glance out the back window to see missiles whizzing towards them, hot on their trail.

~

Carl ran through the woods, grinning as he pictured himself dribbling past the entire team and finishing a slam dunk. With the help of Joe, of course. Carl did the dribbling, and Joe provided the height. As Carl dusted the last player, Joe threw him into the air, soaring into the bucket with the ball.

Carl opened his eyes again, remembering that he was sprinting through a forest, trying to lose the angry bear that was chasing him down. Or at least, he thought it was a bear. He didn't really take the time to examine its features and behavior, he just took off running. The creature seemed smarter and faster than your average bear. He was able to not only chase Carl across the woods, but dictate where he went next to flee. Eventually, the evil creature chased Carl away from Malevita's headquarters and up a tree. Carl breathed heavily and nervously, staring wide eyed back down at the creature. What he had originally thought to be a coat of brown fur was a thick layer of dark purple spikes, allowing the monster to continue to pursue his prey up the tree. Carl launched sharp and explosive weapons and bombs down at the ugly monster, but he only caught them in his mouth and swallowed them in one bite, remaining unscathed. Carl watched in horror as the monster showed off his sharp fangs, almost smiling a toothy and taunting malicious grin.

Carl's mind raced with fear and panic as he scrambled higher in the tree, running out of branches to hide behind. The monster was catching up, about to munch on Carl's left shoe when suddenly, his blood red eyes turned a neon yellow, and he robotically retreated back down the tree, stepping in a straight path in one specific direction.

That was the oddest thing Carl had ever seen, but he told himself that there would be even weirder things happening where he was about to go. He was a runner. An explorer. A courageous warrior. An all star basketball player. Well, he wasn't sure how the last one would help him fight Malevita, but he summed up all of the courage and curiosity he could muster, and he decided to follow the hideous monster that had just tried to attack him.

~

Marta and John were sitting in a pile of leaves at a safe distance from Malevita's headquarters, but the colossal building was still in sight.

"It's your fault if we get poison ivy," John pointed out. After all, it was her idea to make the pile of leaves.

"Oh, shut up!" Marta laughed as she threw a handful of leaves at her brother. He was always the instigator and the one to start the argument, but she was always the one to end it.

But John always put up a fight. He scooped up more leaves and dumped them over her head. The leaves crunched and tore as they immaturely destroyed their neatly organized blanket of camouflage.

Suppressing another burst of laughter with her final toss, Marta declared, "Alright, alright, that's enough! You win."

John stopped throwing leaves and instead fixed their neat pile. When he finished, Marta was still trying to pick the remaining leaves out of her long brown hair. As she extracted the last leaf, she heard a rustling noise behind them. Her heart started to race.

"What was that?" she whispered to John. "Did you hear that?"

"Hear what?" he asked in a normal, loud voice.

She shot a warning look towards him and got up to investigate. He followed her and they looked around for a possible source of the sound, but didn't find even the smallest of chipmunks.

"You were probably just hearing things, Marta. Let's go back to our post," John concluded.

"Yeah, even though I can't believe I'm saying this, you're probably right."

They sat back down and Marta spotted an open window on the first floor. *That's odd,* she thought. *It's almost like they* want *us to go in there!* She thought about it more and realized that it was exactly what they wanted. That must be the room containing Malevita's mind control machine. If they tried to go in, their minds would be warped, and they would be helping perform Malevita's evil will. But if they could send something in there that would destroy it, a third of their mission would be completed!

"John, don't you have that long range bow and exploding arrow that Joe gave you?" Marta asked him.

"Yeah I think. Why?"

"Look," Marta pointed to the open window.

"We can get in!" he jumped up excitedly.

"No! That's what they want us to do. If we go in that way, she'll wipe our minds! That's probably where her machine is! We can destroy it with one explosive arrow!"

"Let's do it!" John pulled the arrow back, aiming at the open window.

"Let it fly," Marta declared.

As he released it, something jumped out at him and bumped his arm, throwing his aim totally off target. The arrow launched straight up out of the bow at a very high trajectory with no forward distance. Marta, John, and their attacker looked straight up as they watched the flaming arrow rise and fall right before their eyes. It erupted, blowing the life out of the dead forest.

~

Chapter 25

Joe quickly found his flame extinguishing tool as he tried to stop the missiles. Mark jerked the controls and the copter nose dived at the last moment, barely clearing the first missile. The other one followed their trail and Mark had to spin the copter off to the side to avoid the other one.

The missiles sped on by, crashing through the sky, hopefully to land in water far away from any inhabitants, but they would never know where they ended up.

"Where will they end up?" Mark nervously asked. His impassive expression finally showed an emotion: Concern. For the good of the innocent people who were possibly in danger of getting injured because of the missiles.

"I don't know Mark, but we have to keep going. It's not our main concern. Our mission is to reach Malevita's headquarters, and that is exactly what I intend to do," Joe spoke bravely. He pointed to the trail of smoke left behind from the missiles and they followed it until they were hovering above Malevita's headquarters, searching for a way in from the top.

Joe's communication device startled him. "Tim to Joe: I found a secret door on the roof of Malevita's building! It's above some sort of information room with special top secret files of some sort. You know the side with the woods that we came from? It's on the opposite side of the building, but it's concealed by what seems to be a roof garden."

"A garden? Why would someone like Malevita have a garden?" Joe asked amusingly.

"That's beside the point, Joe!! Just try to find it okay??" he pushed. Joe reflected that Tim never allowed himself to relax and laugh a little. He was always too intently focused on the task at hand.

"Roger that. Mark, get us in a little closer, will ya?" Joe asked. "Tim says there's a secret door."

Mark glided the copter down, closer to the building.

"There it is, I see it!" Joe exclaimed, pointing out the copter window towards a small vegetable garden.

"Uh, Joe? That's a garden," Mark pointed out.

"Yep," Joe nodded like it was a totally normal thing. He didn't say anything else.

Mark looked at him questioningly. "A *garden* door," he repeated skeptically.

"And?" Joe beamed.

Mark wasn't sure if Joe was pulling his leg, or if Tim was trying to play a prank on them. Either way, he didn't believe it, but he steered the copter towards the garden anyway. As Mark leaned forward to corroborate the discovery, a laser jet of green light jutted towards them. Mark quickly jerked the controls, swerving the copter out of the way, missing the laser by a few inches. Another laser fired, and Mark was ready this time. He dodged the copter out of the way, plunging right into the top of the powerful forcefield. Electricity zapped through the metal copter, stopping the blades from spinning. Mark desperately tried to gain control of the falling copter, while Joe was screaming at the top of his lungs. There was nothing they could do to soften the fall, so they braced themselves for hard impact.

As fear and sadness rushed through his body, Joe realized that they had one last chance. Since the copter took the meat of the electrical shock from the force field, they were still okay. That wouldn't last long, but they could at least try to evacuate the copter and land inside the secret entrance.

"Mark, open the hatch door!" Joe commanded.

"What??! Are you crazy??! We'll die!" Mark yelled. Now he was showing a lot of fear, but then again, who wouldn't?

"We're gonna anyway, just do it!! We don't have much time!" Joe shouted back, his heart pounding and his stomach lurching.

Mark did as Joe said, and they prepared their parachutes. As the copter was approaching the building, Mark and Joe leaped out, barely making it out before the copter erupted in flames on contact with the building. They braced themselves for hard impact as well, but it never came. They were falling and falling into an endless pit of darkness.

~

"Alex to Rose: There was a significant breakthrough in the security! The electrical force field is malfunctioning, we have control of the security cameras, and the concentration of guards in the front area has decreased by over half! Now's the time, Rose!"

"Rose to John: Should I go?"

Rose waited for an answer, but he didn't respond. She nervously thought about the perpetual list of terrible things that could have happened to him and Marta, but she pushed them out of her head. She had to focus all of her thoughts on making the right decision. She didn't like the idea of entering the unexplored building right after something exploded on the roof. But then again, like Tim had said, now was a great chance to get in! Rose had the perfect angle, and she could take on anyone, even if they were three times her size.

~

Tim looked on his screen featuring the view from the video cameras inside and outside of the headquarters. Guards were frantically rushing to the roof, to investigate the damage that Mark and Joe had caused. He knew that they had been trying to look for the trap door he had told them about, but didn't know if they had made it before the explosion. He looked at his camera screens and didn't spot either Joe or Mark.

"Tim to Joe: Do you copy?"

No response.

"Tim to Joe: I repeat, are you okay?"

Still nothing.

"Tim to Mark: Do you read me?"

He didn't respond either.

~

Rose quickly organized herself and prepared to plunge into the dangerous enemy base.

"Rose to Alex: Am I clear?"

Alex viewed all angles of the cameras and spotted tons of guards on the roof. At the front, there were only five. Besides them, there was nothing between Rose and the headquarters.

"Five guards out front. Besides that, you're clear to go."

"Alright, thanks. It's now or never," Rose said as she prepared herself to sprint, but waited for a hesitant minute.

"Alright, you coward, get out there!" Alex encouraged.

And so she did, burning with extra anger from Alex's insult.

Rose ran out from the woods, exposing herself to the guards. One immediately saw her and pointed.

"Hey you kid! What are you doin' here? Go getter, Muscles."

The big guard next to the one talking pounded his fist into his other hand and closed in on Rose. She ran right towards him and ducked as he swung at her. He towered over her like a sequoia tree, and she crawled right underneath him, taking out his legs. She kicked the other guard and darted around the other three men, causing them to dizzily watch her shoot across the area in circles. She finished them off using her specialized gun that Joe gave her that made her job unique. It had multiple settings including set back, stun, knock out, and finish, on multiple different levels of attack such as electricity, bullets, fire, and a few other things she didn't know all that much about, but she was dying to try out. She proudly snuck in through the front door, coursing with excitement, confidence, and a bunch of nerves.

~

"Mark? Hey buddy, where are you?" Joe shouted.

"Over here!" Mark waved his arms but Joe couldn't see him in the dark.

Joe heard Mark's voice echo through the chamber and he followed the sound. He occasionally bumped into tables and boxes, and as he walked, something crinkled beneath his feet.

"Ow!" Mark remarked as something hard ran into him.

"Oh, sorry! Guess that's you!" Joe laughed.

"Where are we?"

"I don't know, but we have to be in the headquarters, right? Where else would we have fallen?"

"I think you're right." Mark clicked on the tiny flashlight that Marisol gave him. He frowned at the small light it produced.

Joe laughed. "Try this, man." Joe handed Mark a small light device, that didn't seem like it had much more power than Marisol's small toy. But when he clicked it on, light filled up the room, revealing the many cabinets of books and files, and the paper scattered on the floor.

"It must be some type of information room! What a lucky first try!" Joe exclaimed. He picked up a piece of paper on the ground. It had a top secret red seal stamped on the top of the paper, and there was a name and a picture of some random guy. A shivering chill shot through Joe's body as he glanced at the short paragraph about "who this guy was" and another larger paragraph about "who he is now."

Mark went to communicate to Tim about their interesting discovery, but his device was scorched from the explosion. Instead he took a picture of one of the files using a tiny but good quality camera Adella had implanted in the sleeve of their uniforms and sent it to Tim at the fieldhouse control center.

"Tim to Marisol: Mark and Joe's communication devices are shot, but I just got a picture of a file from them. They must be okay. I think they made it through the secret door."

"Thank goodness!" Adella exclaimed as she overheard Marisol's message. She was relieved that they were okay.

~

Carl lost track of the creature, but he didn't care. He had reached his destination. His mouth gaped open as he waited in shock just outside of the mammoth building. He stood there excitedly, trying to decide where his fun would begin.

He spotted the purple monster again, entering the mastermind headquarters through a large door that seemed to recognize it. The door opened for a short amount of time, and Carl knew his time was limited. Without thinking about possible risks, Carl darted after the monster and slipped through the "doggy door."

Once again, Carl had to admit that he was impressed with Malevita. She had some pretty wicked stuff. He was inside a decent sized room, filled with strange creatures and monsters lurking in the shadows of their cages. The glowing eyes, growling snarls, shrieking screams, stiff heat, vile stenches, and slimy gloop intrigued Carl. He was intimidated yet fascinated by these amazing monsters that he had never seen before, even in horror movies or fantasies. But shortly after he realized that the cages were unlocking, one gruesome thought filled his brain. It was feeding time, and he was between them and their food. No, he *was* the food.

~

CHAPTER 26

Chapter 26

Rose was completely and utterly baffled as she looked around the room. This was supposedly a top secret headquarters for an evil mastermind, and yet she was in a room with a soft rug, a warm fire, a comfortable couch, and a large grandfather clock that was rather comforting. Rose collapsed onto the couch by the fire, allowing herself to take a moment and relax. She thought about the last time she enjoyed some time resting, and traced her past all the way back to when her father used to live with her and her mother back at the cottage. This memory took over her thoughts and she could only think about the good times with her parents before her dad left them.

The cozy room faded away and was replaced by a small area with a wooden kitchen table. Three people were seated there, singing and celebrating. There was a charming man and a beautiful woman, both enveloping the small girl in an affectionate hug. Rose remembered the scene perfectly. It was her sixth birthday, and her family was celebrating with a rare and special treat of cake. As they finished singing the song, her father stood up as if to say something important.

"Make a wish on this very special day, Rose! Happy Birthday!" he praised.

The young girl paused for a second, tightly closing her eyes and crossing her fingers. She then took a deep breath and blew as hard as she could, but only extinguishing three of the six candles. She tried again and they blew out, the light fading away.

Rose sat up on the couch. She remembered exactly what she had wished for: An adventure. And right now, she was definitely in the middle of a pretty big adventure.

But there was one thing that she realized now that she didn't think of before. *Why was that day "very special"? Was my dad planning to leave? Did he already know that my sixth birthday celebration was the last moment we would have together as a family and that he was reminding me to never forget it?* She wondered. *Why did he leave us? We were so happy together!* Rose wanted to feel angry about her father's mysterious disappearance, but something told her that he did it for a good reason.

The room was making her feel calm and cozy. She curled up by the fire and her eyelids grew heavy. She gave in to the sudden exhaustion that had taken over her body and she drifted off into a deep sleep.

~

Marta sat up after the blow to find the guard beating up her brother. She tried to pry the guard off of him, but he simply shook her off and continued to beat up John. Pain shot through her own body, but she could only imagine the pain John was experiencing. His face was bruised and bloody and out of her love and determination for John's well being, Marta tried again. This time she succeeded in tearing the attacker off of John, but he only proceeded to beat her up next. She knew that she didn't stand a chance against this guy. Her strength was her quick thinking, and being good at puzzles and codes wasn't going to stop this guard from beating her up. Paralyzed by pain and fear, Marta was defenseless. John weakley took out the first weapon he could find and he stunned the guard. Marta saw the the guard go limp, and she rolled out of the way before he collapsed on top of her.

"Thanks John. I owe you one," Marta whispered as he helped her back onto her feet.

"You said it!" he exclaimed.

Marta rolled her eyes. "Let's get in there."

"Marta to Tim: Are we clear to enter?"

"Which door are you using to get in?"

"An open window on the first floor on the north side of the building," John answered before Marta could, telling her with his eyes that it was their only chance to get inside.

"Okay I'm looking at the cameras and I see a lot of books inside the room; you'll like that Marta!"

She smiled.

"Any guards? What about big scary machines?" John pressed, eager to change the subject, not to mention get away from the dangerous area where the guard had attacked them.

"No, John. I don't see any guards. And no, this is not the room with the mind machine. You're going to have to try a little harder for that one. I don't see it on any of my cameras. But watch out for traps! I see laser and motion sensors on the windows, but I'll take care of those for you. There could be more, so just watch out okay?"

"Thanks Tim. Tell us when you shut down the motion sensors," Marta stated.

"Done," he replied quickly.

Marta looked impressed. John rolled his eyes. "Let's go," he confirmed, with no hesitation or concern in his voice.

They lightly sprinted up to the building and dove through the window before they could be spotted by anyone else.

Marta gazed at the endless shelves of books in wonderment. "Wow! Tim was right. There are a lot of books in here." She took one off of the shelf and opened it, half expecting something to blow up or jump out at her, but nothing did. She excitedly flipped through the pages, captivated by the suspenseful story.

A loud bang startled Marta, tearing her out of the pages of the book. She looked over to see the bookcase flat on the floor, the books scattered around the ground. And her brother was standing right next to it with a concentrated smirk.

"John!" she shouted, appalled at what he had done to the books.

"What?" he asked innocently, "Don't mind me."

"How can I *not mind you* when you're making tons of hullaballoo that's sure to alert someone of our presence?!!"

"I'm looking for a secret doorway. Or a staircase," he replied as he knocked over another giant bookcase.

She winced as it slammed to the ground, but decided that her brother might be onto something. "I'll help you look, but don't make so much noise! Someone could easily find us if you keep this up."

"Alright," he agreed. They slid the bookshelves out from against the wall, not finding a secret door, latch, or staircase of any sort. John sighed disappointedly. He was really hoping to find a secret room that would have the mind control machine, and he would destroy it and save the world. But things just didn't work out that way.

Marta sat down at one of the tables and continued reading. John stared at her disapprovingly.

"What?" she replied defensively. "Reading helps me think."

John shook his head and moved on to the next curious thing in the room: The Grandfather clock. It seemed ancient, yet had not a trace of dust on it. He examined the pendulum, the clock face, the roman numerals, and the ticking gears, when suddenly the pendulum swung wildly, the gears rotated quickly, and the hands spun out of control. He threw his hands in the air and took a big step back.

At the sudden noise, Marta looked up from her book and her eyes grew wide. "WHAT DID YOU DO?" she shouted.

But before John could plead his innocence, two strong guards seemed to have popped right out of the clock, knocking John onto the ground.

She pulled out one of the weapons Joe gave her and fired it at the guards. Surprisingly, they both doubled over, joining John on the floor. She helped her brother up, and they looked at each other, gleaming with the same strange idea. John reached to the back and spun the gears as fast as he could. The hands whirred and John and Marta reached out and touched the glass face of the clock. They had no idea what would happen next, but they went for it.

And they would later regret it.

~

"John to Tim: Find a room with a grandfather clock!" he shouted urgently.

"For what?" Tim replied curiously.

"Just do it!" John shouted back.

To Tim, it sounded like John was being thrown around recklessly, so he just decided to follow his command. He looked through his camera to the rest of the rooms and noticed a large grandfather clock in every one.

"There's a clock in every room! What about them?" Tim shouted back, wanting to know the reason for the antique object to be hidden in the corner of every room.

"That must be how you travel from one room to another! They're some type of portals or doors or something," Marta reasoned.

Tim heard a thud and a high pitched shriek just before he heard static and the connection broke. The whole clock thing was rather strange, but he assumed that Marta was right. Since he wasn't sure if Marta and John's devices were malfunctioning, he decided to send the report to the rest of the team.

"Tim to all: Marta found out that the grandfather clocks in each room are portals! They are the doorways from one room to another, so try and investigate!"

John scowled as he heard Tim's report. "Where's my credit??"

~

Carl heard Tim's message just in time. The beasts were enclosing on him, and he frantically looked around for a grandfather clock. To his surprise, there was one sitting in the far corner of the room. It seemed strange for a nice clock like that to be in such good shape while sitting in a room with monsters, but he didn't complain. He tried his best to jump over the snarling creatures and sprint to the clock. As he was spinning the gears, a monster sunk his sharp fangs into Carl's right leg. He winced as pain shot through his body, but he continued to manipulate the gears on the clock. The room swirled and disappeared, the monsters with it. He was floating violently on a gust of whipping wind, and eventually slammed on hardwood floor.

He slowly got up, grimacing as he tried to put weight on his wounded leg. He looked around to see an elegant dining room with a fancy table cloth and velvet chairs. He saw the shining silverware and pure white china dishes that he proceeded to ignore, and kept looking around for what he was really hoping to find.

And then it hit him. The delectable aroma of freshly baked garlic bread wafted through the air and directed him towards the gigantic buffet of delicious foods. His mouth watered as he gazed in wonderment at the plentiful supply of greasy pizza, buttery pasta, soft chicken, fresh fruits and complicated desserts.

For some miraculous reason, all of the pain in his leg washed away, and all that he could think of was: *What do I start with?*

He ran back to the table to snatch a plate and load it up with everything that would fit. Running out of room for his desserts, he grabbed another plate to satisfy his sweet tooth with mouth watering cream puffs and delectable brownies. His plate was overflowing with his favorite foods as he sat down and dug in.

Boy, Joe's really missing out! Too bad for him! Carl thought as he shoveled spoonfuls of chocolate pudding into his mouth. He had scarfed down multiple servings of a variety of foods, chomping and slurping with an enormous grin on his face. And when he could no longer stuff anything else into his stomach, he dropped down and did 20 push ups, before eating another piece of delightful pie. Finally, he set down his fork in defeat, and leaned back in his chair.

Eating such a delicious meal reminded him of past Thanksgivings at Joe's house, where they would eat an exquisite meal, and play an intense ping pong tournament against the relatives.

Then a sudden thought made him tense up with worry. He had forgotten that he was in Malevita's headquarters! Why would she have a feast set up? Unless...

A guard appeared out of thin air and pointed a small ray towards Carl. "Caught you red handed my boy!" he chuckled maliciously.

Carl looked down at his hands. They were covered in spaghetti sauce.

But that was the least of his troubles.

~

CHAPTER 27

Chapter 27

Rose woke up with a start as she heard Tim's message. But someone else had heard it too.

The guard glared at her with a twisted smile. "You can't try to get past me shrimp! I'm not letting you get away!" he shouted as he held up a complicated ray gun.

Rose whipped out her contraption, countering his attack with one of her own. She noticed his hand was starting to shake, revealing the slightest bit of fear. She used this to her advantage.

"You scared to hurt a little girl, tough guy? You'd better be! I'm feistier than you might think!" she announced as she took a brave step closer to him.

"Trust me, I think you are pretty feisty. But no match for me!" he grinned, exposing a few missing teeth.

Rose shuddered on the inside, but wasn't going to let this guy see her fear. She adjusted the settings on her gun to "knock out," but before she could press the button, a warm wave of emptiness swept through her mind like a calm wave crashing on the peaceful ocean.

~

Marta had no time to think about how strange it was for a clock to be a portal into another room. No time to think about their mission. No time to think about what craziness was going on.

She could only think about the horrific images dancing around and taunting her. They were wispy images of her worst nightmares, and yet they seemed so authentic. She could hear nothing but the moans of her dying brother and the uncontrollable sobs of her mourning his loss. She tried to look away and block out the terrible scene enveloping her, but as she closed her eyes, the haunting images fogged up her head. She couldn't escape the terror that was so suddenly and unjustly thrust upon her.

John looked over as Marta was hunched over sobbing. "Marta! What happened? Are you okay??" he asked shaking her slightly to try and wake her up from some sort of trance.

She continued to tremble violently, balling her eyes out, when suddenly, she disappeared. John blinked a few times and looked at the spot where his sister was, but she was no longer there. Horrified, he turned around to see Agent Polythize, the evil criminal and murderous killer from one of John's favorite television shows. He had always been deathly scared of Agent Polythize ever since he was five, and had had bad dreams about him ever since. He loved the show, but Agent Polythize scared him to death, especially since there were rumors about his criminal record in real life. He didn't believe them, or some of them at least.

Past nightmares and gory images flashed before his eyes, and he couldn't believe what was happening. He tried to defend himself against Agent Polythize, but the criminal was too experienced. John was attacked and his world went painfully black.

Only then did he realize what was happening.

Marta had been crying because she was seeing a nightmare, just like he was. He realized with a shudder of fear that Malevita must have been controlling their weak minds, and they couldn't do anything to stop it.

John snapped back into reality around the same time Marta slowly stood up and wiped the last few tears from her eyes. She saw him and her face relaxed with relief and she suddenly rushed to his side and enveloped him in a gigantic hug. He hugged her back awkwardly, trying to be supportive, but failing. He felt a warm tear drop and splash on his shoulder as Marta cried out.

"You were gone! I lost you! You were gone, John! I couldn't bear it!" she sobbed.

He felt a pang of guilt as Marta's nightmare played through his mind. She had dreamed that he *died*. She loved him. She was scared for him. And all he was scared of was a stupid fictional villain. *Well, possibly fictional.* John corrected himself. But then he felt bad about it all over again. It didn't matter whether the rumors about Agent Polythize were true or not; his sister cared about him, and he had done nothing in return.

"It's okay. I'm here now. We're together," he comforted, but it wasn't enough. They were empty comments with no meaning, and he knew it. He wished there was something more he could do for his sister.

~

"Hurry up, Mark! We can't be seen!" Joe whispered as he jumped up, out of the room and back onto the roof.

"Not everyone has extreme hops like you, Joe! I don't play basketball anymore!" Mark shouted back as he tossed up their giant stack of files. They were trying to take as many files back to fieldhouse as they could, so that they could ask Tim to find the people affected and try to bring them to fieldhouse so that Nysoum could restore their memories. Mark climbed on top of a table and jumped up to grab Joe's extended hand. Joe pulled him up to the roof and they tried to furtively run across to the other side. It didn't work out too well.

"Hey you guys! Freeze and put your hands up!" a guard shouted as he started to chase after them.

Mark stopped and turned to look back. Other guards were closing in.

"What are you doing, man?!" Joe shouted, noticing that Mark had stopped. Joe just grabbed him and kept on running. With the files in one arm and Mark in the other, he couldn't do anything else.

"Put me down, you idiot!" Mark shouted to Joe. He set Mark down a little too roughly and quickly used a grappled arrow to latch onto a tree in the woods. Before Mark could even get back up, Joe grabbed him and jumped off the roof, swinging into the forest and away from the attacking guards.

They landed forcefully onto the ground, but they were okay. Joe let go of Mark and they continued to run for their lives, back to the fieldhouse.

"Let us in!" Mark shouted.

Tim looked on his fieldhouse security cameras and noticed Mark and Joe standing impatiently at the door, holding a great big stack of manilla folders.

"If you insist," he joked, unlocking the doors. But only Alex could hear him.

When they entered the tech room, they showed the files to Tim and Alex.

Alex looked concerned. Tim burst out laughing.

"What's so funny?" Joe asked ignorantly.

"You realize that I could have *easily* hacked into Malevita's database and retrieved all of these files, right?"

Mark groaned.

"You're kidding me!" Joe shouted angrily.

Adella and Marisol came rushing in. They heard all of the shouting and came in to check on the runners.

"I thought I recognized your voice!" Adella smiled, looking toward Joe.

He ignored her. "I can't believe you, Tim! There was no need to come back here, then!"

"I'm glad you did," Marisol added. "I can keep track of you two trouble makers again." She handed each of them a new communication device.

"Thanks," they mumbled, still frustrated that they had to lose their ground at the headquarters.

"We can fill you in on the things you missed," Adella suggested. "Mart-"

Tim cut her off. "The grandfather clocks in each of the rooms are the portals, or doorways, to the other rooms."

"Oh okay. That's a good thing to know," Mark said, cheering up.

But Joe wasn't paying attention. "Is Carl alright?" he asked hopefully.

"I think so. Actually, I'm not sure. I haven't heard from him in awhile," Alex answered.

"Oh," Joe sighed.

"You can try to contact him, though!" Tim added. "As a matter of fact, I'm going to make a call, too." He got up and left the room.

Mark frowned. He had an idea who Tim was going to talk to.

~

"Tim to Marta..." Tim announced, hopeful that he would get a response.

"What's up?"

"May I have a quick word? Is John listening?" he asked, slightly indicating that he wanted to talk to her alone.

"Anytime," she replied sincerely, "but whatever you have to say to me can be said to John, too."

John refrained from smirking. Marta knew how to talk with authority. (Even though Tim would probably do whatever she wanted anyway.)

"Alright," he conceded and pulled up a map of Malevita's headquarters and found the roof garden secret entrance. "Right now I'm looking at the secret door that I guided Mark and Joe through."

"And?" John asked impatiently.

"They're back. They brought stacks of top secret files with them."

"About what?" Marta asked nervously.

Tim avoided her question. "The room underneath the secret door must be their information archives, where they store all of the files."

"That's fantastic! We can show these to Nysoum so that he can restore these people's memories," John suggested.

"That's what I was thinking," Tim pointed out, trying to show that he deserves the credit for the idea. "And what do you think about it Marta?" Tim asked. "I wanted to ask you before I told Nysoum."

"Oh yeah, it's all about Marta. Not like the decision maker's sitting right next to her or anything!" John muttered.

"I don't think it's such a good idea," Marta answered, ignoring John's comment. "Isn't it a *little* bit of a coincidence that the room they *happened* to fall into was the second most important one?"

"Well, yeah. I was thinking that too-"

"Don't you think Malevita is smarter than that?"

"Yeah-" Tim agreed.

"So you think they're fake!" John interrupted.

"Exactly. She's trying to trick us. I think she must want us to change these people's minds to what she claims they used to be, but they're really just what she wants them to be!"

"She's trying to use us?" Tim asked nervously.

Marta nodded slowly, not that he could see her anyway.

~

When he returned, Tim announced that he had discovered something.

"I was having a discussion with Marta, and-"

"Knew it!" Mark muttered angrily.

"What's that?" Tim asked, raising an eyebrow.

"Nothing."

"That's what I thought. Anyway, *Marta* thought that the files you guys found are fakes. And that Malevita is trying to get us to change these people's minds to "what they used to be," which is really just what she wants to change them to! We can't let her use us! We have to find the *real* files. Mark and Joe, *Marta* and I think it would be best if you went back to headquarters," Tim put emphasis on her name out of spite towards Mark's attitude.

"And what does John think? *He's* decision maker, after all," Mark snapped.

"He agrees," Tim replied matter of factly. "And Marisol and Erin? We need you to go there, too."

Their eyes widened with fear, but they accepted their new positions for the benefit of the team.

"We'll be back soon, Dell. I promise," Marisol assured as they left for Malevita's headquarters. But little did she know, she would be breaking a promise to Adella for the first time ever.

~

CHAPTER 28

Chapter 28

Danny had been helping Nysoum without any doubts for quite some time now. He helped him design his mind machine, plan fieldhouse events, and do many housekeeping jobs around fieldhouse. Handling Rose and Kylie and Eric would fit in that category. He considered himself to be a loyal and trustworthy staff member, but there was one thing that troubled him. Nysoum had been acting strange lately. He sent the kids and other staff members off to do the mission in Malevita's headquarters, and that was the mission, wasn't it? But then why wouldn't Nysoum be helping? Instead, he had asked Danny to stay out of the Malevita mission and help him with his own personal jobs. Danny helped him without any argument, but now he was starting to question Nysoum's actions. Why would he start a great big mission, and not help with it? And if he was planning to restore people's minds, why wasn't he perfecting the possible flaws in his machine? Danny continued to help Nysoum, but he decided to watch him a little more closely.

~

Before her discussion with Tim, Marta couldn't bear to be in that room anymore. John had found the clock hidden in the shadows of the corner, and they time traveled through the clock. They had no idea where they would end up next, but they decided that it would be better than the room that they were in. Either the room was designed to vividly project your worst nightmare, or Malevita was controlling their minds. Both were gruesome thoughts to think about. They drifted off into the whipping time breeze, and they were used to it this time. They floated around the portal of time and landed softly on the tiled floor of a new room they had never seen before. It was a large and spacious room, filled with weapons and machinery whirring and clicking with life, yet it had a cold, empty feeling. Before they could investigate the technology, Marta heard Tim call her on the communication device. That was when he had asked her about the files that Joe and Mark found. After she thought about it, she knew that they had to be fakes. Malevita wouldn't put the real files in a big room, stacked up right below a secret entrance, just waiting to be stolen.

Knowing that there were still real files out there along with Malevita, and possibly many mind warped people, Marta felt stressed. It helped a little to know that she wasn't alone, and more teammates were coming to help investigate. She knew that Rose and Carl were already in the headquarters, even though she hadn't heard from them in a while, and Joe and Mark would return to keep looking. Marisol and Erin would be coming soon too, to try and help look for all of the things they needed. Marta's complex and overwhelming thoughts were abruptly interrupted by John.

"Woah!!" he shouted with fascination. "Look at all of this stuff!"

Marta snapped out of her daze and ran over to see what John found. He was looking at blueprints for some type of complex machinery ray. Her eyes grew big as she noticed the complicated settings and astounding capabilities of this ray. Then something hit her. Malevita didn't make one gargantuan mind machine; she was planning to create multiple little tiny rays that still had the ultimate power of one big one. Each diminutive ray could distort, wipe, or replace someone's mind. Painful shivers shot through her body as the heavy truth set in. As she flipped the blueprint over to the back, there was a 30x marked in chalk white marker. Next to it was a thick red check mark. The rays were already completed, and probably lurking in every shadowy corner of this haunted headquarters.

John had already moved on to the next thing, messing with all of the other machines like an excited little boy in a toy store.

"What's wrong with you John?" Marta asked, appalled.

He looked up from his complex technology. "What- what do you mean?" he replied helplessly.

Marta immediately felt guilty for accusing him. She could tell how wounded he was, just by her few words.

"I'm sorry John. I didn't mean it like that. I just- I don't understand how you could be playing with this stuff when we have so much that needs to be done, and not much time to do it. And Malevita's ready, John! She's going to attack us at any time know, any place, too! The rays just screw up everything!!" she shouted angrily.

"I know Marta," he agreed softly, "but I'm not playing around." John threw the contraption into the air and picked up something else that looked like a small remote. As the object started to fall, he suspended it in the air, controlling it with the little remote. He pressed a button and fiery sparks exploded from a cannon.

"Oh, sorry! That's not what I meant to do!" John laughed as Marta ducked and covered her head.

John then hit another button where it lowered to hover just above a small ruler, and it quickly scanned it. In the blink of an eye, the machine created another copy of the ruler.

Marta was astounded. "That's amazing John! How many did you find there?"

"Only one, and I call it!" he responded quickly. "But look what else it can do!"

The little machine hovered over the newly created ruler and scanned it. It immediately recognized that it was a fake copy, and reported this to John in the form of a blinking red light. He then chose to obliterate the object by clicking another button, and the copy was gone, leaving only a small pile of ashes on the table.

John thought about everything they needed to do on their complicated mission. They needed to find the mind devices, destroy them, defeat Malevita, and restore all of the minds she had warped. This new machine would help them tremendously.

"Wow, that can be extremely helpful! We can know what's real and what's a fake copy, and we can make fake copies ourselves!!" Marta shouted a little too excitedly.

Someone must have heard her. The grandfather clock in the corner whirred to a fast speed, the hands whipping around as if they would soon burst from the clock face. But they never did. Instead, three large guards popped out of the clock.

"Enjoying our little invention, are you, kids?" The guard shouted to John and pulled out a weapon of his own. It was a small ray that sent shivers up his spine. The minute he saw it, he knew exactly what it was. The mind machine that Nysoum had been talking about was not an "only one big machine" kind of thing. There were a bunch of them, and here was the proof. The blueprint was only the beginning. The rays had indeed been created, and one was pointed directly at him.

"Go," he whispered to Marta. She shook her head stubbornly.

"Hey! No talking!" The guard shouted and held his gun firmly in front of John.

"Sorry, sorry, I'm done," John replied loudly, subtly motioning with his head for Marta to go ahead without him.

"No you're not!" The guard argued.

"Yes I am," John countered.

"Then why are you still talking?"

"Because I'm answering your questions."

"STOP!"

"Okay," John replied easily.

The guard held the ray higher, daring to shoot. "You don't think I'll shoot this, do you?"

He only needed a little more time. "Yes I do."

"AARRGGH!" The guard went to fire the ray, but Marta pushed him from behind, and he landed flat on his face. John had been stalling so that Marta could slowly move out of the guard's field of vision and attack him. They quickly tied up the guard, trying to prevent him from attacking again. Marta swiped his mind ray and tried to use it on him. Her hand shook as she held it in front of his face, and she slowly dropped her arm.

"I can't do it John! I just can't. Malevita's evil for using vile machines like this, and I won't stoop to her low level!" Marta shouted.

"You're right," John nodded. "But how are we going to stop this guy from escaping?"

Marta's eyes gleamed. "I think I have a pretty good idea," she declared with a smile.

~

"Erin? How do we get in??" Marisol asked, her voice trembling with fear.

"I- I don't know," she responded with a similar quavering voice. "But there's gotta be a way, we just need to find it!" she said, cheering up their frightened spirits with a simple smile.

"You're right," Marisol agreed, gaining courage with every step.

When they arrived at the evil headquarters, Marisol noticed a sensor that was guarding a high portion of the brick wall, that seemed like it could open like a secret entrance if properly triggered.

"Erin! Try to set off that motion sensor. It might open up to let us in!" Marisol pointed to the brick wall.

"Okay," Erin replied with a confident nod. She cartwheeled up to the building and flipped into the air, triggering the motion sensor that pushed one brick out and onto the grass. Erin picked it up and saw a sequence of five letters, a sequence of five numbers, and a sequence of five picture symbols.

"Mary, come over here! You've got to see this!" Erin whispered excitedly, trying not to draw any guards to them.

Marisol came over to look at the brick, but by the time she saw it, the designs disappeared. "I don't see anything but an old brick."

"What? That's so weird! I saw numbers and pictures and letters, I swear!" Erin stated.

"I believe you...Maybe they're asking you to repeat the characters like a code! Do you remember any of them?" Marisol asked.

"A few. But what do I do with them?"

"Try drawing them back on the brick!" Marisol suggested, handing her a sharpie from the gap in the wall where the brick fell out.

Erin didn't make any move to start drawing.

"What's the matter?"

"I'm no artist.." Erin mumbled.

"That doesn't matter! We just need you to write the letters and numbers you remember, and try to draw the pictures as best as you can!" Marisol encouraged.

"Okay," Erin replied uneasily as she tried writing down what she remembered, and guessing on the others. "Done!" she replied, showing Marisol her masterpiece.

"Great! Now put it back in the slot and see what happens."

Erin slipped the brick back into the slot and for a second, nothing happened. Then suddenly a few bricks fell out randomly. Marisol picked them up but there was nothing on them.

"What if each brick fell for each character that was correct? Take it back out and see if you can try again on the ones you missed," Marisol advised.

Erin yanked on the brick that was loose before, but it was sealed tightly to the rest of them. There was no trying again. They had to deal with what they had.

Marisol took out a small catapult and fired a stone through the small, vacant holes left by the fallen bricks. She heard it make contact with something a ways inside, and knew that if they could make the hole bigger, they would be inside the headquarters.

"Step back Mary. Watch out." Erin warned as she fired an explosive into one of the small openings. As it erupted, the bricks from the secret entrance crumbled, and they ran into the headquarters.

They found themselves in a rotating room that spun around in different directions and gravity was a little off. They tried to float around in the odd room, trying to find a grandfather clock that would take them to a different room. This one obviously wasn't any help to them.

‿

Malevita sat in her velvet red throne chair. She could sense the enemy's presence. So many young, naive children, waiting for someone to warp their minds. She heard another explosion behind her by the secret brick entrance, but once again did not lose her cool. Instead she waited for the two girls to come to her, and then she would be ready. She held her personal ray and as the two girls landed hard on the tiled floor of her throne room, she aimed it at the first one. She started to distort her mind, and an even greater thought formed in her brain. She didn't have to take down every single member of the fieldhouse team; she could use these two, and whoever else her guards encountered, to destroy them from within. But as she finished up the first girl, the other one found the grandfather clock and escaped.

No matter! Malevita thought. *One is a good start.*

"Meg!" Malevita beckoned one of her many henchmen.

"Yes master?" Meg replied as she entered the room and obediently stood by Malevita's side.

"How many do we have?"

"Three."

"Three is perfect."

~

CHAPTER 29

Chapter 29

"John to all: I have something extremely important to tell you when we get back to fieldhouse. Get out of here as soon as possible! See you then!"

~

"Did you hear that message, Rose?" Carl asked.

"Yep," Rose replied with a loathing glare. "It was from the traitors. The enemies. The evil ones!"

"Let's go back and DESTROY them!" Carl replied.

"Good plan. Lead the way."

"Hold up guys!" Marisol shouted.

They looked back at her, unsure if she was on their side.

"I'm with you. Ready to defeat the evil Noa Nysoum!" she shouted.

Rose and Carl nodded their heads in approval as the three of them marched back to the fieldhouse.

~

"Glad to see that everyone made it back safely," Nysoum reported when everyone gathered in the main assembly room.

Safely? The runners who went in were nearly killed! Or worse, possibly brought to Malevita's side through her mind distorting rays. I can't believe he could call it safe!! John thought angrily.

"Although Nysoum thinks we're safe, we're not! Malevita has multiple little rays that are just as deadly as the one big machine we had pictured. She can get us anywhere now!" John reported.

Nysoum shook his head, "Thank you Mr. Ivanson, that is *enough*! You don't need to tell us any more we already know."

"What? You already knew this and didn't tell us? Are you *trying* to get us killed?!" Joe shouted angrily.

Marta knew why. He was angry that his machine was not as clever as Malevita's. And he was *especially* infuriated because he thought that his machine didn't work because Rose returned. Nysoum could be keeping even more secrets from them at this moment. Marta reconsidered her opinion of Nysoum's values. Maybe he wasn't so reliable and honest.

~

John couldn't fall asleep; he was too shaken up from the shocking day. He was wide awake when he noticed that Rose, Carl, and Marisol were up and about. What were they doing? He saw them holding the same small ray that the guard had been holding in Malevita's headquarters and his palms grew sweaty. He tried to control his faster breathing and stop his pounding pulse, but he couldn't. Dark thoughts of betrayal bounced around in his head. *Rose, Carl, and Marisol betrayed us! They're spies! I can't believe it! What will they do to us? What do they want from us?*

He turned around in his bed, hoping the noise would deter Rose, Carl, and Marisol. No such luck. They continued to slip along the wood floor in his direction. The floorboards creaked, but they did not seem to notice or care. They were a foot from his bed now, and his muscles tensed. But surprisingly, they didn't stop at him. They walked along, one more bed to his right: Marta. John leaped out of bed.

"Don't touch her, you traitors!" John shouted as he jumped on Carl's back.

"Hey! Get off of Carl, John! You're the enemy! You're the traitors! You sent a bomb at us!" Rose argued.

"What?" John whispered. He was shocked. Who sent a bomb at them? Are they not the spies, and they're just trying to find who is? They had the rays, though. It had to be them, and John knew that his only chance to protect his brain was to sacrifice someone else's, and that was *not* something he was willing to do.

Then, something hit him. Marisol, Carl, and Rose were most likely brought to Malevita's evil side because of her rays. Their minds were probably warped, and the whole bomb thing was just something that Malevita made up to make them think that Nysoum was bad.

John knew that Nysoum was the only person who had the power to restore their minds, and he wanted to go warn him. But before he knew it, he was holding a ray of his own, pointing it at his twin sister.

~

Malevita was listening in as her newest recruits, Marisol, Carl, and Rose, were taking down the entire fieldhouse team. And they deserved it. She promised herself that anyone affiliated with Nysoum would be converted to her side, or annihilated.

This was her vision. This was her revenge. On the man who tried to destroy her vision of a better world. A perfect world. An equal world.

~

CHAPTER 30

Chapter 30

Now working for Malevita in her headquarters, the fieldhouse team thought they knew the truth. They now thought that they needed to do what they could to stop Noa Nysoum.

"'He has another device! You know that? He is trying to distract you with his memory machine instead of showing you his real thing!" Malevita lied.

"And what is it?" Carl asked with excitement.

"I don't know, but it is *not* a joke," Malevita glared at Carl. "You know everything you need to know. You have everything you need to have. Now you just need to do some investigating. He is defenseless. He has no guards. He has no support. He has no teamwork. And he has no heart. But he does have secrets, and we need to uncover them."

"So what's the plan, boss?" Marta asked looking to John.

"Excuse me, but *I* am in charge here. And anything Nysoum told you is now officially over!" Malevita enforced.

John nodded to hide his expression of relief. He was glad to have the position of decision maker lifted off of his shoulders.

~

The entire fieldhouse team except Nysoum and Danny was now on Malevita's side, thinking that it was the right team from the beginning. They packed up their weapons and rays and trudged off into the woods to go back to fieldhouse. When they arrived, Tim and Alex easily hacked into the system because they had created it, and they entered their old "home."

Danny heard the voices as his former friends were terrorizing the building he had worked at for many years, and decided to do something about it. He assumed that Malevita's ultimate goal was to destroy the selective memory device, and probably Nysoum with it. He knew that in no time, the kids would enter the room with the selective memory device. And when they did, he would be ready. He and Nysoum had been working on amplifying the device so it could work on multiple people at once, within the range of the room.

In the few remaining minutes he had before the kids came into the memory room, he faced a great internal conflict. He never tried to control the machine before, but he had a feeling it would be relatively easy, since he saw Nysoum use it on Rose. But the real trouble was that he had two options. He could delete every lie that Malevita placed in their heads to ensure that they will stay on Nysoum's side. But was *he* sure he still wanted to be on Nysoum's side? This he didn't know, and it made him want to restore everyone's minds to the way they used to be, before anyone messed with them. Choosing to turn on Nysoum was an extremely difficult decision for Danny, but he knew that it was the way it should be. As he came to this conclusion, he realized that Nysoum was still in the room. He wouldn't be able to use the machine if Nysoum was still here!

"Mr. Nysoum, both you and I know they're here, and they're after two things. You and your machine. It wouldn't be smart to have both of those things in the same place, now would it?" Danny asked, leading Nysoum to the thought that he should flee.

"You're right! I'll see you soon," Nysoum declared as he scurried out of the room.

The minute he left, the door broke down. Danny froze everyone in their motions of attack as soon as they barged into the room. He cleared all of the lies implanted from Malevita, and he restored the rest of Rose's memories that Nysoum had taken away. That had seemed so long ago.

When Danny was finished, everyone looked around in confusion. The only person who understood what had just happened was Danny, and he quickly explained the whole scenario.

"Noa Nysoum's not who we think he is," Danny concluded. "We need to get out of here, and we don't have much time. We don't have a place to go, either."

"Yes. Yes we do," Mark grinned.

Everyone packed up their things and followed Mark out of fieldhouse and through the woods. He led the way to a big mansion with a courtyard garden, and a beautiful fountain statue.

Everyone looked at each other in shock as Mark declared. "Welcome home!"

"What?" Rose exclaimed, unbelieving. "This is *your* house?"

"Indeed it is!" Mark replied with a gleaming grin of pride and accomplishment.

Marta gazed around in amazement. "It's beautiful Mark!"

His cheeks turned a shade of deep pink as he caught Marta's eye, then quickly stared down at the grassy lawn.

"Yes Mark, thank you for being *so generous* to share this small and humble abode!" Tim snapped sarcastically.

He immediately regretted it when Marta glared at him disappointedly.

"Well, let's get inside and get started!" Adella cheerfully changed the subject.

Mark led everyone inside to his family room, with an enormous flat screen television and two puffy and cozy couches. Carl and Joe dove onto the first couch, claiming two of the four spots. Alex and Danny took the other two. John sat down with Marta on one side, Rose on his other, leaving one remaining spot next to Marta. Tim hurriedly sat down, leaving Mark to grumpily sit on the ground with Erin, Marisol, and Adella.

Everyone relaxed and regrouped, trying to brainstorm ideas on how to stop the enemy. But who even was the enemy anymore? Everyone was too tired to think, and everyone dozed off except for Marta and John. Marta tapped John on the shoulder and motioned for him to get up and follow her into another room. They found a game room filled with exciting video games John never even heard of. His eyes lit up as he looked around to try and decide which one to play first when Marta stopped him.

"John, who's the enemy?" she asked, knowing her own answer and wanting to know his.

"I don't know, but any man who tries to destroy the world by warping everyone's minds and trying to blame someone else seems bad to me."

"And what's your opinion on Malevita?"

"I think she was just trying to stop Nysoum."

"So you think that evil woman is good?" Marta verified in shock.

"And you think Nysoum's good? He's bad and you know it!" John accused.

"And so you assume that means Malevita's good?"

"Yes, that's exactly what I think! She's only trying to stop Nysoum!"

"Oh yeah, sure. AND DESTROY THE WORLD!! How can you not see that? You're just as good as brainwashed."

Marta's words crushed John like a weight, stinging him like a hive of angry wasps. He turned away from her in shame and hurt as he started to play one of Mark's video games.

Chapter 31

Marta and John's loud yelling woke Adella up, and she found her way to the kitchen where she made a meal for everyone. If they were as hungry as she was, they would need a lot of food. And so a lot of food they had. Mark and Erin came in after a while and they helped put together fruit, sandwiches, yogurt, salad, and cookies for everyone to regenerate before the ultimate battle.

When everyone was awake and full of energizing food, Marta started the conversation that everyone was waiting for.

"Alright everyone! I would like to pose to you the real question that I'm sure we're all trying to find an answer to. Who is the enemy here, and who can we trust?"

"I'd like to start off the conversation with the fact that Noa Nysoum is an evil man who wants to create a better world by wiping everyone's memories. Despite our prior beliefs referring to his honesty and good visions, he is the enemy," Danny declared definitely.

Rose sat quietly. She remembered the truth about Nysoum, but decided to keep it to herself. She couldn't believe that her kind and loving father turned into this crazy abomination who wanted to take over the world by warping everyone's minds. And plus, telling everyone that Nysoum was her father wouldn't do anything to help them anyway. He was an entirely different person now.

Mark jumped in next. "I told Joe about my friend named Meg, who was my partner back when I did the fieldhouse challenges. She was a great kid, really smart, and really good at sports. But she never made it to the next step after the challenges. Malevita recruited her, warped her mind, and forced Meg to work for her. Malevita has to be the evil one. Anyone who does that to a brilliant girl is truly a villain," Mark concluded.

John wanted to fight back just as he did against Marta, but he knew they were right. They were both evil, and they couldn't work with or trust either person. "I agree," John stated.

"You do?" Marta asked hopefully.

He nodded his head. "I agree with both Danny and Mark."

"What?" Carl asked, confused. "How can you agree with both of them? Someone has to be right and someone has to be wrong! Who's good and who's evil! We need to join somebody's side!"

"You're right Carl. We need to join a side," Joe agreed.

"And we will," Marta concluded. "We will join our own side."

"My computer and I are with you!" Tim declared.

"That's great Tim. Now that she has your computer on her side she feels so much more secure," Rose snapped. "But I'm in too."

"So are we," Adella, Marisol, Erin, and Alex added.

Mark, Joe, Carl, and Danny all agreed to be part of their own team, against both evil mind warping masterminds.

The only person who hadn't agreed yet was John. Marta looked to him with high hopes that he understood that both of these people were their enemies, and they needed to stop them from destroying the world.

"I'm with ya to the end," John promised. "But there's one more thing I wanted to talk about."

"And what's that?" Marta asked.

"We are against Malevita and Nysoum, but they're against each other, too. They're more against each other than against us. We can use that to our advantage. Is anyone really out to get us specifically? Or are they just trying to get each other, and we happen to be bouncing back and forth between sides?" John rushed, his thoughts blurring together.

"Woa," Alex stated, dumbfounded. "Mind blown. Slow down there kid! Can you say that all again?"

John repeated his thoughts, slowing down this time, trying to think about it himself.

"You might be right!" Marisol exclaimed. "What if we step out for a while, and let them fight, trying to take each other down?"

"That might actually work!" Mark agreed.

"I don't know..." Erin questioned. "What if- What if they're not really after each other, and they're trying to- to get us!"

"Nah, stop being a coward. They're not really after us! Why would they be?" Danny stated.

"You know I hate to say this, but I think Erin's right," Marta interjected.

"Hey!" Erin objected.

"Oh, no, I didn't mean it that way!" Marta laughed. "I just meant to say that it's kind of a scary thought."

"Oh okay," Erin replied thankfully.

"So, what do you think Marta?" Tim asked, ready to agree with it before she even said anything.

"I think they are after us, because we're all extremely gifted people. We each have our own talents, and they see us as threats to their "perfect world". They think we're smarter than them and- bear with me here- I think they're afraid of us," Marta proposed.

"What? Afraid of us?" Rose questioned. "I don't believe it!"

"It makes sense to me now!" Mark agreed. "That's why Nysoum invited us to fieldhouse in the first place! He wanted us to be on his side, because he knew that if we knew what he was really up to, we would be against him, and he knew he would lose!"

"So you think Nysoum recruited us to his side because he thinks we have unique talents that he is afraid of?" Adella queried.

"Yep. That's it exactly," Marta confirmed.

"But what about Malevita, then?" Joe asked. "What does she have against us?"

"I don't know for sure, but it might be that she's against Nysoum, and since we were on his side for a while, she is against us," Danny reasoned.

"That makes sense. But what are we going to do about it?" Rose asked, taking their simple conversation to the next level of action.

"We're gonna fight!" Carl exclaimed, excited to take part in the conversation.

"So you said they're after us, right?" Alex asked.

"I think so," Marta replied.

"So what if we get them to come after us?"

"Sounds like a death wish to me!" Joe stated.

"No! I meant to say: What if we leave hints that lead them here, thinking that they will find us, but instead they see each other, and they'll fight!"

"No way! We're not fighting in my place!" Mark shouted defensively, "I just finished remodeling the game room!"

"And the games are sweet!" John added.

"That's beside the point," Adella mentioned kindly. "But I love the idea!"

"So how can we lead them here?" Rose wondered, clearly interested.

"Not here!" Mark grumbled.

"Okay, okay, we get the point. Where should we meet?" Danny asked.

"How about by the lake somewhere in between Nysoum's fieldhouse and Malevita's headquarters?" Erin suggested.

"Sure! We should write a message," Marisol suggested. "It can be coded or invisible ink for authenticity, but we can leave it at fieldhouse and headquarters for them to find and figure out."

"We'll go!" Carl and Joe volunteered.

"Okay, you two go to Malevita's headquarters," John suggested.

"I can go too," Danny offered.

"I'll go with him," Mark declared, trying to show off his bravery.

"You guys can go to the fieldhouse. Drop off the message somewhere you know he'll see it, but not too obvious," Marta advised.

Marta, Marisol, Adella, Alex, and Erin worked on the coded messages. They made them easy enough for Nysoum and Malevita to figure out, but not as easy as Kylie and Eric would need. John was teaching Rose how to play one of Mark's video games, and the other boys were planning how they would leave the messages somewhere to be found.

"Nysoum still thinks I'm on his side, so if he sees me when I go in, I'll say I'm just getting something that I left yesterday, and I'll let the note slip out of my hand right under his computer desk. He'll definitely read it; he's too curious not to!" Danny planned.

"Sounds good," Mark said. "I'll be your backup right outside fieldhouse for whenever you need me."

They took the note the girls just wrote and left for the fieldhouse.

Everything went just as planned. Danny went in, leaving the note tucked in a place that would just catch Nysoum's eye and curiosity. They returned to Mark's house triumphantly.

On the other hand, Carl and Joe decided to slingshot the note in through the window, but it bounced right off. The window wasn't open. The noise attracted a guard to the window, who opened it and climbed out, looking for the boys. He scanned the area, his eyes skipping over the high top prints in the dirt. Carl and Joe held in their breath, trying to be as quiet as possible. Carl was hiding behind a bush, and Joe in a tree. Not the best hiding spots, because if the guard looked up, he would immediately see Joe, and the bush concealing Carl was small with patches containing nothing but a scrawny and bare stick.

As the wind blew the pollen through the air, Joe's nose twitched. He tried to hold in in, but he couldn't. Joe sneezed as quietly as he possibly could, which was still sort of loud, but miraculously, the guard did not hear him. Joe pumped his fist in celebration, swaying and shaking the tree branch. A leaf broke off the branch, and it slowly and silently floated to the ground. Joe hoped that the guard wouldn't notice the leaf, but it fluttered down, landing right on the guard's head. He swept it off with one fluid and strong movement, looking up to see what could have caused the leaf to land on his head, because it wasn't fall yet! He spotted Joe immediately, aiming his weapon up into the tree.

This gave Carl enough time to slip out of his hiding spot and toss the note through the open window. Once the job was done, he shouted and screamed, hoping to bring the guard's attention to him. It worked! He saved Joe! But then he realized that he brought the problem to him. He ran straight towards the guard, leaping over him, kicking his shoulder just before they collided. The guard toppled over off balance and rubbed his shoulder. He rotated it a couple times and then quickly leapt back up. But Carl and Joe were quicker. They ran away as fast as they could, through the woods and back to Mark's house.

~

Chapter 32

"Malevita, I found something you might just be interested in," Meg offered.

"It better impress me," she warned.

Meg showed Malevita the note.

"And what might this be?" Malevita smirked.

"A note from the enemy, leading us right to their new base! We can find them and fight them. After all, they're the only talented kids left for us to... change."

"Thank you Meg. I will go. Alone. You stay here and hold down the fort in case it is a trap for them to come and destroy our headquarters," Malevita ordered.

Little did she know, it *was* a trap, just not for that reason.

~

Nysoum had seen the paper slip out of Danny's hand, but was not about to tell him about it. Danny was acting a little odd lately, and Nysoum had his suspicion. The note was surely the key to answers. Once Danny was long gone, Nysoum reached under his computer table and opened the note.

It was in mirror code and cursive, which was never his strong suit. He found a mirror and did his best to read the flowing cursive.

Danny,

I found what I needed from the database archive computer. Meet the rest of us at the lake at twelve o'clock noon tomorrow.

~Erin

"The rest of us" alluded to the fact that his entire team of kids would be there, and he could go there and get them back on his side. But when was tomorrow? Was that today? Did he miss it? He would never know for sure, but he had to take advantage of Danny's foolishness. He would take his chances.

~

Chapter 33

Sure enough at exactly twelve o'clock noon the next day, Nysoum and Malevita showed up at the lake. Expecting to see the kids, they were shocked to see each other and immediately took out their weapons, ready to fight.

From their spot in the woods a ways behind the lake, John watched in horror as his eyes darted back and forth, like watching a ping-pong match. From Nysoum to Malevita. Nysoum, Malevita. Evil to evil. He didn't know which team to root for. It was like two foreign sports teams playing each other, except this time he cared who won. He didn't want either team to win.

"Are we just going to stand here?" Rose asked irritatedly. She was eager to jump in the action.

"What else can we do?" Adella asked helplessly, "We can't jump in there without our minds getting destroyed!"

"You're right," Tim reasoned. "Marta and I'll stay out of the fight and work on creating something that will repair everyone's minds."

"No way!" Marta and Mark shouted simultaneously.

"I'm not missing the fight!" Marta assured.

"And who knows how productive you two will be!" Mark retorted.

"And what's that supposed to mean?" Tim asked.

"Oh nevermind!"

"I'll stay with Tim," Alex suggested. "After all, I'm the other computer genius!"

"Okay, good plan. I know you guys will do great!" Marisol praised as Tim and Alex retreated back to Mark's house.

John looked around at everyone, so eager to fight against the two evils, and stand up for what they knew would be justice. Carl nodded curtly. Joe beamed. Danny rubbed his hands together. Adella and Marisol tied back their long hair. Rose took out her gun with a small grin. Erin stretched her arms. Marta looked up at John.

After a minute passed, John realized that they were all looking up to him, waiting to be summoned to battle. He grinned back at them, taking out his skateboard. He hadn't ridden it in a while, but now was a great time to crack it back out. He threw it on the ground and glided toward the plunging battle of minds, leading the team of unique people, each with their own talents and strengths.

"If you forget everything else, just remember your own talent. Use it against them. That is why you're here. That is why Nysoum is afraid of you," Marta advised.

And so they plunged into the battle immediately feeling insane. Their minds fogged and twisted and they suddenly couldn't remember who they were, why they were there, and what they were doing. And then the next instant, they were crazy kids who had been working for Malevita for 10 years.

"Yes! Yes! Get him!" Malevita exclaimed as she noticed that all of the kids were slowly drifting towards him. She pointed at Nysoum and they swarmed him like a hive of irritated bumble bees.

"NEVER!" Nysoum shouted as he suddenly wiped every memory back away from the kids.

Rose didn't know where she was, or who she was, but as she felt herself fly around the group of people fighting, she knew she was quick. She ran up behind the evil woman and swiped her ray.

"Hey!" Malevita yelled angrily.

Rose giggled, tossing the ray to Danny, who crushed it underneath his large foot.

"Take that your evilness!" Joe shouted as he hopped over her attempted missiles.

John skated up to Nysoum, circling around him as Marta tried to confuse him with crazy genius questions that only she would know the answer to.

Adella, Marisol, and Erin used their strong teamwork and cooperation to shut down Nysoum's machine while Marta and John were distracting him. The mind machines were gone, now they just needed to stop the masterminds. Carl threw a rock at Nysoum, his perfect aim hitting him square in the knee, causing him to limp. Joe slide tackled his other leg out from under him and Nysoum went down. Danny held his arms and legs in a tight lock, keeping Nysoum from moving. Rose held her gun out in front of him, knocking him out for a good while.

One down, one to go. Mark thought. He ran over to Malevita and tackled her, just as he had done in high school football before Nysoum had recruited him at the fieldhouse. Adella, Marisol, and Erin all helped to hold her down as Rose knocked her out as well. They had defeated the evil masterminds!! At least for now.

‿

Chapter 34

Back at Mark's house, Tim and Alex created a special memory device based off of Noa Nysoum's old machine, and restored everyone's minds. Tim tried to use it on Malevita and Nysoum as well, changing their evil minds for good. But of course it didn't work.

As punishment, Marta advised that they sent the evil masterminds back to the confines of their own buildings. Alex and Tim reactivated the challenges back at fieldhouse, where Nysoum would have to face his own creations. They also hacked into Malevita's system to ensure that her traps were still set up, giving her a taste of her own medicine.

The next step was to find all of the people affected by both Nysoum and Malevita's rays. Tim hacked into their websites to find names and addresses of people who were mind warped by Malevita and Nysoum. Not to his surprise, they all had one thing in common: Special talents. Tim, Alex, Adella, Marisol, and Erin stayed at Mark's house to keep looking for victims of the mind machines, while Marta, John, Rose, and Danny all went to find and restore these people's special minds.

Mark, Joe, and Carl all went to Malevita's headquarters to restore the guards' minds and allow them to return to their normal lives. Aware of Malevita's presence, they carefully traveled from room to room by grandfather clock. Mark looked for one guard in particular. He found her working in the technology and machinery room and his heart raced.

Tim could have Marta; he had Meg now. Mark quickly restored Meg's mind and asked her to join their team. She willingly accepted, excited to return to her real life full of adventures.

~

"What do we do about Kylie and Eric?" Rose asked.

"We're restoring everyone else's minds, so we should probably restore theirs," Marta reasoned.

"I don't know though. It might be better if they stay ignorant to the entire fieldhouse thing," Danny suggested, feeling guilty that he had helped warp their minds in the first place.

"No, we have to fix them. Let's go," John decided.

~

Once everyone returned to Mark's house, he asked Meg to help him prepare a victory feast for the team. Everyone loaded their plates with crunchy vegetables, warm, fluffy breads, and spicy tacos.

"Thanks Mark and Meg! This food looks delicious!" Adella praised.

"I'm glad you like it," Meg replied kindly.

"Let's dig in!" Mark declared.

Everyone sat down around his large dining room table and John and Marta praised everyone's efforts at the big battle. "Great job today everybody! We should all feel really accomplished and proud of our great team efforts against Nysoum and Malevita, and now we can celebrate as we share a great feast that Mark and Meg have graciously prepared!"

Everyone stared down at their plates, filled with food waiting to be eaten. Rose dug in first, and everyone followed, chowing down on the delicious food.

"Why does this seem familiar?" Carl asked, puzzled. "Wait a second..."

"What man?" Joe asked.

Carl set down his fork and pushed back his half eaten plate.

"What's wrong?" Joe queried again.

"The last time I had a feast like this, one of Malevita's guards came in and wiped my mind!"

"What?" everyone asked, having no idea what Carl was referring to.

Meg burst out laughing. "I know what you're talking about! One of the rooms in Malevita's headquarters was a dining room with a buffet of steaming food. Did you fall for it?"

He nodded his head shamefully.

"Don't worry Carl. It's not a trap this time," Meg assured after laughing some more.

"Oh, good!" he exclaimed and dug in once again.

"Ready for dessert?" Mark asked, bringing in a platter of warm cookies, gooey brownies, and scrumptious pies.

"Woah," Alex muttered as her mouth watered. She stared at the delectable pastries, waiting to snatch a few.

"Thanks Mark!" Marisol said as she served herself a brownie and passed down the plate.

"Anytime. Well actually, not anytime, but maybe one other time," he declared with a smile, looking around at the table full of friends.

~

"So now what do we do?" Rose asked, after they finished their celebration feast.

"I guess we go back to our old lives," John sighed.

"Easy for you to say! You're a middle school student! That was a while ago for me," Alex announced.

"Yeah, I don't really remember where I worked before fieldhouse," Danny agreed.

"We'll go back to playing professional basketball," Carl and Joe declared, sharing a grin.

"Don't you two kid yourselves, you're still at the middle school, too," Marta stated. "And Tim, drop by every once and a while to say hi, okay?"

"Will do."

"Where do you guys go to school?" Erin asked Adella and Marisol.

"Oh we go to a private catholic school, but it's not far from Tim's high school."

"And how about you, Rose?" John asked curiously, "What will you be up to?"

"I'm finding my dad, and going back home to live happily ever after. Wouldn't that be nice?" she asked rhetorically.

"Well Meg, I guess we'll go back to being best friends and sports rivals!" Mark laughed.

"Nobody forget this," Marta advised as a few last words of farewell.

~

CHAPTER 35

Chapter 35

Rose found Nysoum back at fieldhouse. But something was different about him. He wasn't Noa Nysoum anymore. He was Roger Hillary. As soon as she saw him she knew that he was her father once again, and she rushed up to him and embraced him in a giant bear hug.

"You're back! I knew you would be!" Rose shouted.

"You found me. I'm so proud of you! You were so great during the challenges and so brave during the final battle! But I want to tell you something very important. It's a confession for why I left you three years ago. I guess I have to go all the way back to when I used to work with Malevita, who still went by Mallory back then, and a girl from Springville. We worked at a top secret underground facility for the government, trying to design a selective memory device because they wanted to create a perfect world where everyone was equal. Once we did as they asked us to, we left the agency, and I discovered that the perfect world would never exist and as we keep trying to strive for perfection, it will only grow worse. Everyone has their own talents and that is the way it should be. But Mallory- now Malevita- was trying to develop something that would wipe away everyone's special talents, and replace them with terrible things that I can't even imagine. So I left you three years ago to build the fieldhouse empire for talented and gifted people like you. I left so that I could protect you and other gifted people from Malevita and her evil vision," Roger explained.

Rose could hardly hear what he was saying. She finally knew the truth about her father and his disappearance. He left to protect her, and he was never really evil! After all, he never did anything to hurt anyone (except Kylie and Eric). *Wait a second!* Rose thought. *Why would he invite Kylie and Eric to the fieldhouse if they were truly that dumb? What if they were actually really smart and Malevita had warped their minds to remove their talents, and replaced their skills with stupidity. He was truly trying to reverse what Malevita did!*

"And what about Kylie and Eric?" she asked, hoping that she was right.

"Malevita got to them before I invited them to fieldhouse. They were very musically talented, but Malevita stole their gifts before I could protect them. And yes, that is why they were so- below the level of the other competitors. So to try and counteract Malevita's wrongdoing, I tried warping their minds. Who knows if it worked..."

"We fixed them along with the other people Malevita destroyed," Rose declared proudly.

Roger nodded his head in gratitude.

"Come on, Rose. Before we head home I want to show you something!" Roger took her outside the fieldhouse and lifted her into a go-cart. "During the challenges I noticed that I never taught you how to ride a go-cart. Let's do it now!" he exclaimed, eager to have a fun time with his daughter after many years without communication.

~

"Go Carl, GO!!" Joe shouted to cheer on his friend after he set the perfect pick.

They were playing basketball against the best team in the league, and they were losing 38 - 42. Carl had the ball, and he dusted the first defender, drove down the court, and took it in for a layup.

"YES!!!" Carl exclaimed as he did a small victory dance.

"Hey! Get back in line Carl! It's not over yet!! We're still losing!" their Coach shouted.

They set up a man to man defense, guarding each player very tightly. The point guard on the other team took it down the court, and Carl pressed him to make a quick decision. He threw the ball all the way down to another player, but Joe stole the pass.

"Yes Joe! Go! Quickly!! Ten seconds!! Five, four, three...!" Coach counted down.

Joe stopped dribbling in the middle of the court.

"WHAT ARE YOU DOING!!!??" Coach shouted angrily. "DON'T STOP!!"

Joe launched the ball forward from half-court. It soared through the air, and swished right into the basket for the three points they needed to win.

"Joe! Joe! Joe!" the team chanted as they rushed onto the court and lifted him onto their shoulders.

"Great team effort, guys! Way to get the win!" The coach shouted, looking directly at Carl and Joe. They had scored every single point their team had on the board, and were the only two superstar players. The rest of the team was terrible, so Coach's comment about the team effort was really only directed to Carl and Joe.

"Three cheers for Carl and Joe!!"

"Cheer! Cheer! Cheer!" The team shouted as they fell over laughing.

That was how they celebrated Carl and Joe's outstanding performance in every single game. The Hip-Hip-Hooray thing got a little boring, so they improvised.

"As team captains we thank you guys for working so hard this game to beat our big rivals. After five years of losses, we finally took them down!" Carl announced.

"Cougars on three! Three!" Joe shouted.

"COUGARS!!" The gym rang with enthusiasm.

The team cheer was louder than ever, and Carl and Joe felt great to be back in the game.

~

"Good morning, Mr. Holland!" John remarked cheerfully.

"Welcome back John. Glad to see you're alright. Did you get the homework I sent home to you?"

"Homework???" John asked uneasily.

"Yes. I gave Susanna Luckran a few pages to drop off at your house. Did you not get them?"

Oh, phew! Only a few pages. "Oh no I didn't. I'll check again tonight."

"That's alright. I'll give them to you now before class starts," Mr. Holland offered. He walked over to his bookshelf behind his desk and pulled out a five ton history book with an entire binder full of worksheets and notes waiting to be filled out. He handed this stack of work to John and he almost fell over.

What?? You call this a few pages?? John thought. "Thanks," he managed.

"This can be due two days from now."

What??!! Are you kidding me??? How generous!!

"I was going to make it tomorrow, but in case your internet is broken, I'll give you another day."

"Internet?" John asked.

"Why yes, did I forget to mention your 3 hour documentary?"

John's jaw dropped and he walked away. When he set his things down, the desk collapsed onto the floor.

"John, would you please stop destroying my classroom?" Mr. Holland instructed.

John's face turned bright red. "Sorry," he replied lamely.

"Alright class. Let's begin right where we left off. Ancient history of Rome," Mr. Holland announced. "Open your textbooks to page 37."

"Here we go again!" John muttered, unconsciously tapping out Morse code on his desk.

~

Within the first day, Tim had already made up all of his school work from the time that he missed. He still had perfect grades in all of his classes, and felt that he had learned the material five years ago. In every class, he sat at his desk, falling asleep with boredom, while all he could think about was the mind games, physical tasks, and computer programming he did for the past month. And he had to admit, he sort of missed it.

~

Adella and Marisol were president and vice president of their school student council. As soon as they returned, they discovered that Silvia had been trying to take over their positions. She scheduled meetings and was about to start up the monthly fundraiser without asking anyone. When Adella and Marisol found out about this, they called a meeting to discuss the monthly fundraiser with everyone on the council.

"Hi everyone," Marisol began. "Sorry Adella and I have been out for a while, but we're ready to hear *everyone's* ideas for our monthly fundraiser."

"What do you think about a bake sale?" Silvia quickly introduced her idea.

No one really said anything.

"Yeah, maybe!" Adella responded kindly. "But how about a mini Olympics? We can have lots of athletic events out on the track, the football field, the baseball field, the pool, and some academic events in the school too," Adella suggested.

The council jumped on that idea.

"Yeah!"

"Let's have a few events each month that all contribute to the overall Olympics!"

"Sounds great!"

"Will it be individual or team?"

"We could do it like the real Olympics, where you have each person compete individually, but to represent their country."

"Okay! We can split everyone up into teams for Countries based on their athletic, academic, artistic, and musical abilities to make the teams as even as possible," Marisol added.

"Alright, so it sounds like we have two main- great- ideas! Before we vote, does anyone have any other ideas?" Adella asked.

No one really answered.

"Okay then. Heads down!"

Everyone except Adella closed their eyes and put their heads down on the desk.

"All in favor of the bake sale," Adella declared.

One hand went up. *Silvia's no doubt.* Adella thought.

"All in favor of the Olympics!"

Everyone else put up two hands to show their excitement.

"Only one hand guys! I have to count," Adella instructed. "Okay! So it looks like we'll be having the First Annual Bridgewood Academy Monthly Olympics!"

The council cheered. Even Silvia seemed a little excited.

Adella and Marisol took their idea to the principal, and he accepted, excited to try something new and original in his school.

As enthusiastic as Adella and Marisol were, they knew the Bridgewood Olympics wouldn't be as fun and intense as the fieldhouse competition and the ultimate battle of minds.

~

"Don't make me go back in there alone!" Rose pleaded. "She's different! Ever since you left she's been so sad. She couldn't leave the house without thinking of you and feeling lonely."

"Just do it Rose! I promise I'll knock on the door as soon as she closes it again!" Roger promised.

"But what if she decides to... attend to me before she opens the door?"

"Don't worry, I'll make sure she sees my shadow through the window. Do you still have the sweet smelling candle we bought up at town?"

"Yeah."

"Give that to her when you go in. That'll distract her enough for me to come in next. Ready?"

Rose nodded her head and Roger hid just underneath the small cottage window. When he gave her the thumbs up, she boldly knocked on the door.

Her mother opened the door with a harsh glare. "And where did you sneak off to young lady? I looked everywhere for you!"

She looked for me? I didn't know she left the house! "I brought you this candle! It's lavender."

"Lavender?" Mary paused for a second. She knew that Roger used to buy her lavender candles every Friday when he came home from work. And Rose didn't have any money to buy a candle! She could only dream...

Just then, she heard a knock on the door. "Who could it be? No one's ever come here before! Not even salesmen or politicians." Mary's heart raced as she opened the door slowly.

"R-Roger?" she asked in disbelief.

"I'm back Mary! I'm home for good."

"I- I didn't know you'd ever return!" She exclaimed lovingly. "But why did you leave?" she asked.

Roger explained the entire story about Malevita, how he left to create the fieldhouse empire to protect the talented people, and that if he told her then he was afraid that Malevita would do something bad to her.

"So this whole time, you've been fighting for the cause?" she asked slowly and quietly.

"Yes," he replied. "Can we sit outside in the woods? The weather is very nice. And Rose has something for us in her basket."

Besides looking for Rose, she hadn't been outside the house in years. "Oh- uh- sure!" Mary replied, still in shock that Roger had returned with Rose. Their family was united.

Roger unpacked the basket he and Rose filled with food they bought at town and set up a picnic in the woods. They laughed and played just like good old times.

But Rose realized something was missing. The challenges and the mission brought her something she never had before, and she wasn't ready to give that up. The friendship with every person she met at the fieldhouse was very important to her, and she knew that her dad would be up for a reunion. He thought they deserved to know the truth.

~

Science was one of the three classes Marta had with John. But you never would have guessed they were twins. Besides the fact that they looked alike, they didn't sit together, work on group projects together, or even really talk to each other during class. John hung with his friends, Marta with hers. But after the challenges, something changed. Marta and John didn't feel that they were really friends with anyone at school anymore. During their long absence, everyone carried on normally, and now that they had returned, no one seemed to notice or care. John and Marta sat together at their own remote table, but they were the smartest two in the class. They worked on assignments together, and when they finished, they took out something they decided to start working on. It was a floor plan sketch of an enormous training building that they decided that they were going to repair. It might be a while before it could happen, but they were going to fix up the fieldhouse into a training center for their real friends.

~

CHAPTER 36

Chapter 36

Danny had nothing to do, nowhere to go. That's why he was so relieved Marta called him.

"Hello?"

"Hey it's Marta. Is this Danny?"

"Yep."

"John and I have been working on fixing up the fieldhouse to make a training base for us to hang out and prepare for uh- what's coming. Did you hear about it?"

"No, not yet. But whatever it is, I'm in."

~

Every single person returned to the fieldhouse. They were shocked to see Noa Nysoum standing in the corner with Rose close by. Before anyone could ask, he started to talk, explaining the entire truth from start to finish. Everyone realized that Nysoum really didn't do anything bad after all, and he was trying to protect them more than anything else. When he finished his speech, John stood up and started clapping loudly. Marta elbowed his knee, but he didn't stop. Carl, Joe, Danny, and Mark joined in.

After everything he did for us, why are you mocking his speech? Marta thought.

But the girls soon followed with a standing ovation, and the clapping continued louder than an exciting touchdown at the national championship football game. Marta stood up and joined in, only to realize that everyone was clapping, not sarcastically, but as a sign of gratitude, to thank Nysoum for sacrificing his life and his family to protect them from Malevita. Rose's eyes glowed with admiration for her noble father. Her thoughts of abandonment were replaced with pride and excitement. She knew that the two of them and the rest of these unique people belonged together to solve this unique crisis.

"Hey Noa Nysoum-!" Joe shouted.

"Please, call me Roger now," he corrected.

"Roger Nysoum- I mean Roger Hillary- I just wanted to say that I loved the challenges! The competition was really fun!" Joe announced.

"Yeah, I liked it too!" Adella agreed.

Everyone bubbled with agreement about their overall appreciation of the exciting tasks. They all thought that the challenges were difficult, yet exciting, and they were eager to compare their results from each of the individual tasks.

"I'm glad everyone," he responded.

"Speaking of the competition, I think we're going to have to start it back up," Marta suggested.

"And why do you say that?" Roger asked.

"Because the mastermind is at it again."

"What?" Meg asked, "Malevita is still trying to reach her goal of an equal utopia where no one has any talents?"

"Well, sort of. Except she's moved on from people with talents," Marta explained.

"Phew! That's a relief," Carl exclaimed.

"Not exactly," John answered. "Malevita has only expanded her target range. She is going after everybody now. And she's trying to make everyone *extremely* talented, but equal."

"What's so bad about that?" Mark asked. "I wouldn't mind being really good at everything!"

"It seems good now, but if you think about it, everyone will be prowess-es at every single thing, and no one will be special. Every person will have the same abilities, even if they are really good, but it will just seem average!" Adella concluded.

"That's right, Dell! And we have to stop Malevita from corrupting our world once and for all this time," Marta explained.

"So what's the plan?" Tim asked Roger, glowing with admiration and respect for him. Tim was finally starting to realize that he was not the leader of this thing, and was content with being just a team member. Roger was the true leader.

"Don't look at me!" Roger exclaimed. "I'm not the leader. We all saw where that took us... I think I have to pass the leadership to the next generation." He looked down at his small daughter, who jumped up in objection.

"I can't be the leader!!" she denied, "No way!! I choose Marta!"

"Yeah, Marta would do a good job," Tim supported.

"Yes, Marta! You'll be great," Marisol praised.

"Okay, okay. I'll do it," she agreed. "But everyone is allowed to put in their own input, because we're all here together for a reason. We all have our talents, so let's use them."

~

Chapter 37

Marta had been elected leader for all of two hours before the disaster occurred.

Meg, John, and Marta decided to go back to Malevita's headquarters to investigate. They knew it was a risk, but it was a risk they were willing to take for the cause.

Meg was the key to their success. She was dressed as a guard, and still carried her identification badge that opened all of the doors and locks. Holding one twin's arm in each hand, pretending to have captured them, Meg led them through the front door and into the comfortable living room. She knew all of the tricks, and she wasn't going to fall for any of them. Heading straight for the grandfather clock, Meg brought Marta and John into the next room which was one they had never seen before.

Before talking, John made sure that the coast was clear. "Where are we?" he whispered. "We weren't in here before!"

"It's the room where the real files and information are stored. It was designed so that only certain people can access it," Meg explained. She looked around for Malevita, but she was nowhere to be found. "Drat! Since she's not in here, she must be in her throne room."

"She has a throne room? And wait- why are we *trying* to find her?" John questioned.

"Uh, so that we can *stop* her!" Meg replied obviously.

"Oh," he muttered, still feeling quite uneasy about the plan of attack.

"Okay. I'm going to go check her throne room, but I need someone to come for my plan to work. I'll enter the room normally and distract her for someone else to enter through the brick wall and-"

"Enter through a brick wall," John repeated skeptically.

"It's a coded secret door entrance. Which one of you has a better memory?"

"Me!" John exclaimed, jumping up to prove he had some worth.

Meg looked at Marta questioningly to confirm this.

"It's true. He does," Marta sighed, frightened of being left alone in this nightmare mansion.

"Okay so John, you come with me, and Marta, you stay here so that if we both get warped, you can go back to fieldhouse and tell everyone to save us," Meg instructed.

"What? I'm just supposed to leave you guys here at Malevita's mercy and flee?" Marta objected.

"And I'm not leaving Marta by herself!" John agreed.

"It's the only way we can do this," Meg pointed out.

Marta swallowed and decided that Meg was right. As bad of a feeling she had about being left alone, she nodded her head. "Okay," Marta acquiesced. "See you soon."

~

Meg entered the throne room through the grandfather clock and Malevita was nowhere to be found. John casually strode in five minutes later, shocked to see no Malevita.

Meg shook her head. "I don't know where she could be!"

But John had an idea, and it was not a good one.

~

Marta knew it was a bad plan from the start. They never should have only brought three people to the headquarters in the first place, because if they needed to split up, someone had to be alone. And that was precisely the problem.

Marta was looking through files, finding many about random people from towns she never heard of. Malevita was expanding her empire. But then Marta was shocked to see an entire folder filled with files of students from her school. Some of which were her friends. The last straw was when Marta found a folder containing two small but very important names: Her parents. Malevita had to be stopped.

Marta tried to remember the names of the people affected, but not even John could remember all of these poor people who are at the mercy of Malevita's destruction. Just as she was finding more files from her neighborhood, the grandfather clock whirred.

Wow, Meg and John are back already?? Did they beat Malevita that quickly? Marta thought with anticipation and hope.

But Meg and John did not appear out of the grandfather clock. It was the last person she wanted to see.

~

Chapter 38

Carl spotted Meg and John walking back towards the fieldhouse after their mission.

"Where's Marta?" he asked nervously.

Tim heard this and rushed to the window. He didn't see Marta either. "WHERE'S MARTA??!!" he shouted in despair. He ran out the door and everyone followed. Mark and Alex hugged Meg, and Erin, Adella, and Marisol tried to support John and Tim.

"What happened to her?" Rose bravely asked, wanting to know the truth no matter how horrifying it was.

"We were so stupid!!" Meg shouted angrily. "I can't believe we left her alone."

"YOU LEFT HER ALONE???!!" Tim shouted in disbelief.

"We had to. She was looking through the files, and we had to find Malevita," John choked.

"And so what happened?" Joe asked.

"We thought Malevita was in her throne room, so we were putting ourselves in danger. But really, Malevita was somewhere else, and she entered the room with the files when no one was ready. She has Marta now," Meg explained sorrowfully.

"Where?" Tim sobbed.

"She- she left a note."

"May I?" Roger asked.

"Of course," John handed the note to Roger.

A	B	C	D	E	F	G	H	I	J	K	L	M	N	O	P	Q	R	S	T	U	V	W	X	Y	Z

13   5 19 9 6   21 14 17 2   24 6 19 26 6 2

25 13 4 5 14 17 4   5 6 2   21 14 17   19 2 6

17 16 6 24 6 16 16   19 3 26   15 19 4 5 6 4 13 7

13 22   21 14 17   25 19 3 4   4 14   15 2 14 9 6

21 14 17 2 16 6 24 9 6 16   19 3 26

25 13 3   5 6 2   11 19 7 18 '   21 14 17

19 2 6   20 14 13 3 20   4 14   5 19 9 6

4 14   7 5 19 16 6   17 16   26 14 25 3   19 24 24

4 5 6   25 19 21   4 14   4 5 6

16 14 17 4 5   15 14 24 6 .   21 14 17 2

11 6 24 14 9 6 26 '   1 19 24 6 9 13 4 19

"It's a cryptogram!" Roger exclaimed. "I love these!"

"Oh so does Marta," John replied wistfully and started to tear up all over again.

"Well let's get cracking!" Alex exclaimed.

"We know that 8 is a one letter word, so it can only be A or I," Erin deducted.

"And 13 18 is a two letter word used a lot in the message, so maybe it is IT, IS, or TO," Marisol suggested.

"The last word is MALEVITA," Tim blurted.

"How do you know?" Joe asked.

"It is the last word and it follows a comma, so I assume she signed her name at the end of the note. And anyway, it fits," Tim replied matter of factly.

"Alright. That gives us 12 is M, 4 is A, 17 is L, 11 is E, 26 is V, 8 is I, and 13 is T," Roger filled in the letters to spell MALEVITA."

"Now you can use those letters to fill in the numbers that you know in the rest of the message," John instructed.

"Great!" Adella exclaimed. "So we can assume that 5 is H, to make HAVE. And 19 is R to make ARE."

"Nice, Adella," Danny complimented. He wasn't very good with codes, so instead of helping with the deciphering, he decided he would be on the moral support team.

"And you were right about the two letter word, Marisol! It must be TO so 18 is O," Alex suggested.

Roger scrambled to write down all of the letters the team was shouting to him.

"8 23 is a two letter word starting with I, so it's probably IT, IS, or IF. But we know it can't be IT because we have T as a different number," Meg explained.

"I think the first sentence is I HAVE YOUR LEADER," Erin suggested. "It's sad, but true."

"WITHOUT HER, YOU ARE something AND PATHETIC," Tim deciphered.

"IF YOU WANT TO PROVE YOURSELVES AND WIN HER BACK, YOU ARE something TO HAVE TO CHASE US DOWN ALL THE WAY TO THE NORTH POLE," Mark translated.

"I think it's the SOUTH POLE, Mark," Meg corrected, grinning.

Mark looked back down at the paper and a slight grin formed on his rosy face. "You're right," he added.

"The south pole? How in the world are we supposed to get there?" Joe complained.

"I don't know but we'll do it for Marta!" Rose shouted.

"YOUR BELOVED, MALEVITA," John finished. "Ha! Like she's beloved to anyone!"

"So, off to the South Pole?" Danny asked incredulously.

"Yep. Think we'll see Santa, Rose?" Carl teased.

"Shut up you baby!" Rose retorted.

"He's at the North Pole anyway, isn't he?" Marisol pointed out.

Everyone laughed. That was something that they hadn't done in awhile, and it helped to lighten the mood.

"So, any ideas on how to get there?" Erin asked, getting back to the point.

"Well, I used to have a copter..." Mark sighed, remembering his tragic loss on the roof of Malevita's building.

"It wouldn't fit this many people anyway!" Joe shouted. "We need our own private jet!"

"I can probably arrange that!" Tim grinned.

"What? How?" John was flabbergasted.

"I need two people to come with me," Tim ordered.

"No way. I'm not sending anyone in groups of three anymore," John decided. "Optimal number is probably four."

"Sounds reasonable," Meg agreed.

"So like Marta said, we should use our talents," Alex pointed out. "What kind of people do you need for the job?" she asked.

"Good drivers," Tim replied with a small sigh.

~

Mark, Alex, and Danny all followed Tim back to his house. They were the only ones old enough to drive. Erin had a late birthday and was still too young. Meg only had her permit and objected furiously. She wanted to come, but Alex took her place instead.

"It's nothing compared to your's Mark, but here it is!" Tim showed everyone his decently large house with a flourishing garden and a spacious backyard. When he led the other team members around to the back door, he opened his many garages. "This is my collection," he displayed proudly.

"Wow," Mark muttered, speechless.

"That's pretty amazing Tim!" Alex complemented. "But last I checked we can't drive to the South Pole." She looked around at his abundance of cars, her eyes catching the shining, bright coats of paint.

"I know. I'm going to have to sell them," he sighed sadly.

"You're going to sell your collection of these amazing cars?!" Danny asked incredulously.

"Yep. Not even all of these cars put together is worth more than Marta," Tim convinced himself. He knew it was the right thing to do, but it was hard to give up his collection.

"How sweet," Mark chimed sarcastically. "Now let's get moving!"

Tim called the man working at the automobile dealer that he had bought the cars from a long time ago. He told him that they would be coming in with a lot of nice cars to sell and that they would be looking to sell them for a reasonable price. The dealer knew Tim was one of his best customers, and it would probably be a good deal. He accepted the cars and gave Tim, Danny, Mark, and Alex enough money to buy the private jet they needed to go to the South Pole.

~

Chapter 39

"How long until we get there?" Rose asked Roger impatiently.

"Are we there yet?" Carl mocked in a whiny high pitched voice.

"Ugggghh!" Rose grumbled and she unbuckled her seatbelt.

"Rose," Roger said disapprovingly.

"I'm going to talk to John!" she replied.

"No, you're sitting back down," he ordered.

"Fine."

They were interrupted by violent shaking and the plane started to tip to the side.

"Watch out everybody. Hold on tight! We're hitting some turbulence here," Meg explained. She was Mark's co-pilot, and they were already almost a third of the way there with no troubles. Until now. The plane rocked and jolted around and Mark tried to steady it. He concentrated deeply and he finally regained control, navigating through the wind turbulence.

"Mark, we're coming up on some mountains, you might have to increase our altitude," Meg advised.

Mark did as she suggested, leading them through and past the mountain in no time.

"Boy Tim settles for nothing but the best!" Mark exclaimed as he expertly maneuvered the expensive and high quality jet.

"Don't get too cocky," Meg advised, "We still have a little while to go!"

Most of the kids were sleeping, for they hadn't done that in a while. Before, they had been too worried about Marta to sleep, but now they could drift away with the soft lull of the plane engine, knowing that they were on their way to help her. A few of the other kids were doing research, (that was mainly Tim and John) and the others were staring out the window into the sky of empty clouds.

"I see a thunderstorm on the radar," Meg warned. "It's coming in hot! Think we should land it?" She asked Mark, but spoke a little too loudly.

"No!" John and Tim shouted from their seats, determined to reach Marta as soon as possible.

"But it might not be safe!" Meg countered.

"It's alright, we'll be fine. Let's just keep going," Mark decided.

Within 20 minutes, the storm developed to full force. The wind picked up and the rain poured down in a great deluge, bouncing off of the speeding jet. Thunder boomed and lightning cackled in the distance, and they were flying towards it. Before long, they were in the heart of the storm, and every team member was wide awake, sitting on the edge of their seats, with goosebumps and fear weighing them down. Meg was leaning over closer and closer to Mark, trying to loosen his tight limbs and intense glare of concentration. Adrenaline was coursing through his body as he tried to control the jet to make it through the remainder of their perilous journey. The lightning zipped from cloud to cloud, getting ready to strike. As it shot through the sky, Mark could only react to its actions. He was 100% defensive, and had no way to get back at the storm. There was nothing he could do to stop the raging storm around them. An enormous lightning bolt struck within inches from the jet and everyone screamed with dreading and paralyzing fear.

"Land! Land NOW!" Meg shouted, panicking. "We're above the Southern Ocean, close enough, just LAND!"

"AAAAAHHHH!" Mark shouted as he jerked the jet into a sharp nosedive, not caring about the harsh descent. He was just trying to stick the landing. And he would've. If it was above land. But instead, they barreled straight into the Southern Ocean, exploding into smithereens with the unimaginable speeds crashing into the bubbling waves.

Meg was the first to pop up to the surface, gasping for air, searching for their brave pilot. "Mark! Mark! Where are you?" she shouted, barely noticing the other kids scrambling to the surface.

Mark soon kicked up to the surface holding Rose, handing her off to Danny, who was much stronger, and didn't need both hands to tread water. She pushed away immediately because she could swim just fine on her own. Carl, and Joe swam around crazily, lifting up Adella, Marisol, and Erin. Alex and John popped up to the surface shortly after, and Roger swam over to be with Rose.

Everyone was accounted for. Or so they thought.

"Is everybody okay?" John asked as he spit out a mouthful of salt water.

"Yeah I think so," Erin managed.

"Where's Tim?" Alex asked, looking around the bobbing water.

"I don't know. I don't see him anywhere," Adella answered.

"I can't find him either," Roger added.

"I'll look for him!" Joe bravely announced before diving back underwater. It was dark and murky, and he couldn't see a thing. He popped back up to the surface. "It's darker than Malevita's piercing glare down there; I can't see anything!" Joe shouted, starting to splash around frantically again.

"Stop splashing!" John ordered. "I'm looking for bubbles!"

Everyone searched the surface for tiny air bubbles rising. "I see them!" Erin shouted, pointing in the near distance.

Danny power swam over to the area and dove down as deep as he could, hitting into a skinny and limp body. Danny grabbed Tim and lifted him back up to the surface where he coughed up buckets of salt water.

"Thanks," Tim managed. He had to squint to see that his rescuer was Danny, because he had lost his glasses in the fall.

"You alright Tim?" Marisol asked.

"I think so, thank you. I just can't see farther than a few feet in front of me, so don't leave me in the dust."

"Awww," Carl joked, though he was serious. He knew that he was a better swimmer than most of the people in their group, and it would be tough for him not to burst ahead.

"Alright everybody. Let's go. I think we're going that way," John pointed South and they swam towards the endless horizon.

~

CHAPTER 40

Chapter 40

After swimming as hard as they could plus a little bit more, they had to take a break to catch their breath.

"We still have to tread, so the break isn't going to do much. Let's just keep going!" Mark pushed.

"I need a minute," Tim puffed.

"At least," Marisol added with an exasperated smile.

"Fine, but let's get moving soon!" Carl and Joe agreed.

Once everyone managed to control their breathing rate, they knew they had to move on. There was nothing they could do to stop their muscles from aching until they reached land, so they began to swim again, stroking one arm after the other, kicking furiously with all their might.

"Land ho!" Joe shouted after an eternity.

"Come on guys! We can do it!" Meg cheered. She, Mark, Carl, Joe, and Danny were not as exhausted as the others. They were all in good shape and were mainly chosen for the fieldhouse competition for their athleticism. For a nine year old, Rose held her own, and she was helping her father more than he was helping her. The other girls were struggling, but they continued on, knowing that they were almost to land. Tim was falling behind, but his determination to save Marta drove him forward.

John refused to even think about fatigue, for each stroke added to his persistence and will to rescue Marta.

Eventually, the team reached an icy snow covered terrain, where they climbed out of the water and collapsed on the ground in a shaking heap. There, they could lay motionless and rest their aching bodies for a few minutes. The exhaustion was soon swept away by the cold, and if they stayed out in the freezing temperature for much longer, they would die of hypothermia and frostbite.

As Meg shifted her position to shield her face from the cold, she felt something heavy in her pocket. She took it out and discovered that she still had her compass after the crash. "We're here! We made it to the South Pole!" she exclaimed before her lips froze. "They should be here somewhere."

"I see a light!" Rose pointed her small finger to a bright light in the dark distance.

"Let's go!" Carl trudged forward in a full on sprint.

The rest soon followed. Before long, no one could feel their legs anymore, and they hoped that they were still carrying them forward. After what seemed like forever, the light did not seem to get any closer. It was like it was moving away just before they could reach it. But in the end, the light turned into a small hut, where they trampled inside the unlocked door, and collapsed by the warm fire.

"Wake me up when you need me!" Joe announced and instantly fell asleep on the floor.

"He looks comfortable," Carl agreed as he laid down as well. Roger, Danny, Adella, Marisol, Erin, and Alex also relaxed by the fire.

But Tim, John, and Rose would never rest until they found Marta, and they searched the hut until they had the place memorized.

"John? Tim?" Rose squeaked. "I think I found something."

John and Tim came running into the room. "What?" they asked hopefully.

But the minute they saw her, they didn't need a response. Malevita was in the room. Their faces turned pale and sweaty; their minds were racing with adrenaline and disorganized thoughts of hatred and fear. But their number one fear was not for themselves. It was for Marta. Tim and John looked around frantically. To their dismay, she was nowhere to be found.

"Sorry friends!" Malevita jeered in a mocking tone. "You're just a little too late! Time never stops ticking you know! I couldn't wait for you forever, so I had to finish her off."

Finish her off??? What did that mean?? John thought, devastated. *It can't be true. Not Marta!!! No, she's too smart,* he decided. *Too smart for Malevita. And too weak,* he thought darkly, tears stinging his eyes. He knew he couldn't hold himself together much longer. But he promised himself he wouldn't give in. For Marta.

Rose was speechless, glaring straight into Malevita's dark eyes as if she would magically transform into Marta.

Tim was just as melancholy. But he was also furious. "You wretched, evil, dragon's slime!" he cursed.

Rose was shocked at the words that just flew out of Tim's mouth. But Malevita wasn't. She just took the insult as something to make her stronger. She thrived on anger, saying nothing more, knowing that what she had already said was enough to tear apart a brick wall. She just sat there in silence with a creepy and malicious grin plastered on her light face.

Rose couldn't stand it anymore. "What, you don't have anything to say to that?" she shouted angrily.

Still, Malevita kept her cool, empty stare and her ominous smirk. She did not respond.

This intrigued Tim and he took a brave step forward to see how she would react.

She didn't move a muscle.

Tim sucked in a deep breath and straightened his chest as he took another brave step toward Malevita.

Still, no response.

Tim took one last step, visibly shaking with fear as he stood one foot away from the evil woman who had killed his only true friend. He could hear his own heartbeat pounding in his chest and feel his own shaky breaths as they wavered in and out. But after a perpetual and dreading five seconds without any reaction from Malevita, Tim became even more suspicious. He realized that he couldn't feel her breaths or hear the beat of her heart. The only sound he could make out coming from Malevita was a strange and quiet mechanical hum.

John realized it a second too late. Malevita wiped Tim's mind, leaving him clueless on the ground. Remembering the weapon he stole from Malevita's tech room, John pulled it out and threw the droid into the air, controlling it with the remote. He hovered the small machine over Malevita's head and hastily pressed the button. Malevita immediately disappeared into a dusting of tiny ashes fluttering to the ground. When her image flashed away, Tim stood up. Once the copy of Malevita was destroyed, his memory was restored.

Rose stared at John in disbelief. "What *was* that?" she asked.

"When Marta and I were investigating Malevita's headquarters, I found this machine that can create and destroy copies of things. I realized that this clone of Malevita was programmed to do two things: Speak that one phrase, and and wipe everyone's mind. That's why she didn't respond to anything we said or did. But if Malevita really isn't here, then where is she? And- and where is Marta?" John's voice cracked.

"Well... how did the clone get here? Malevita must have been here at some point," Tim added.

"That's true! But how did she get here and leave so quickly? She was here and gone by the time we got here, and Mark's jet was no tortoise," John stated.

"Your right. I don't-" Before she could finish, they heard a door creak open in the room next to them, sending chills despite the warm heated house.

An old man stumbled out of the shadows. "Why are you folks still in my hut?" he asked confusedly. "I thought you left this morning."

What? Who's this guy? And what is he talking about? John thought. Then he tensed up angrily. The man must have been referring to Malevita. They had only missed her by a few hours. *But wait! He had said "you folks" meaning plural. Was Marta still here???*

"Sorry sir," John explained civilly, "but I don't know what you are talking about. We were flying a jet out in the storm and we had to land it in the ocean. We swam the rest of the way here, but we were freezing and exhausted, and we just couldn't go on anymore."

"Then please, warm up! Take some hot chocolate from the kitchen, and blankets are in the basket by the couch," he offered.

"Thank you sir," Tim replied gratefully, forcing a kind smile. Though what he truly felt was sadness and anger. He needed to know the truth. "What were you saying about people leaving this morning?"

"A woman with freakishly pale skin and dark black hair and a little girl with brown hair showed up here this morning. Popped right out of my grandfather clock."

"Really??" John's face lit up at the man's description of what had to be his sister. "Where is the clock?"

"Well before the left, they had asked me to smash by beautiful clock. And then they suddenly disappeared, just like they had come. I couldn't believe my eyes or my ears, but I was too scared to believe them. I wasn't going to tear apart my wonderful clock."

"You still have it?" John asked hopefully.

"Oh, yeah. Why of course. It's in the room next door."

Tim and Rose both looked at John. It was too good to be true. "Thank you sir!" they exclaimed and ran back to the room where everyone was.

The man followed and almost had a heart attack when he saw all of the people sleeping on his living room floor. The kids he had spoken to woke everyone else up and mentioned something like "they're gone" and "there's a grandfather clock in the other room". They thanked him again for all of his help and apologized for their abrupt arrival and departure. They ran into the next room and almost like they had done it many times before, the kids spun the gears on the clock. They disappeared into thin air, exactly like the woman and the girl from this morning.

"What are people up to these days?" the man shouted as he went back to bed, hoping it was all just a confusing dream.

~

Chapter 41

John didn't know exactly how many people could travel through the grandfather clocks at once, but it seemed like everyone was accounted for as they floated around in the time capsule of empty space. Suddenly, they crashed to the floor in Malevita's headquarters.

She was sitting in her throne, cackling maliciously. Almost like she had been waiting for them to arrive.

"You're too late!" she exclaimed. "Look outside! Look at what I have done! Everyone has gathered to welcome you home!" she cackled again, motioning for the team to join her outside.

And so they did.

There was Marta, standing among one of many people, gathered around. John, Tim, and Rose rushed to her, embracing her in a hug that would normally tackle someone. But Marta wasn't normal. In fact, she was a super human. Just like the rest of the people there under Malevita's control.

"You can have your lousy mouse back now!" Malevita boomed. "I don't need her anymore. I did what I needed to. Everyone is outstandingly talented! Except you guys of course," she looked at the fieldhouse team who was starting to feel overpowered. "Show them what you can do, guys!" she shouted, bidding her mind controlled superhuman minions to surround the fieldhouse team.

"No!" John shouted. "We'll show *you* what we can do!"

The people stopped, frozen in their tracks.

"I'm listening!" Malevita cooed.

"I challenge you to a competition to see who is truly the best! The challenges will include sports, academics, music, and art. One event from each category, and a tie breaker if needed. Our fieldhouse team versus you and your mind warped robot minions, but you give us Marta! The way she was!" he added.

"And what will the winner get?" Malevita asked, clearly interested in his request.

"The winner will get to do as they wish, and the loser will flee. To Mars."

"As in the planet Mars?" Malevita confirmed with an evil smirk.

"Yes. The planet Mars," John repeated.

"Okay you've peaked my interest. I accept that little challenge of yours," Malevita declared. And with a click of her ray, Marta was back to normal, running up to embrace John like she hadn't seen him in a hundred years.

Tim flipped his hair and before he could realize what happened, Marta hugged him too.

"Thanks," she whispered before letting go again.

"Alright Malevita. We'll alternate choosing events, and the amount of people needed. You may pick first. Keep track of your own wins-" John was cut off.

"I don't trust you to keep track, so I'll delegate someone from my abundance of talented people. Him. And he is no longer mind warped, you can check. He will keep score."

"She's right," Mark confirmed. "He's an impartial scorekeeper."

"Good. Now my first event pick is a marathon," Malevita smirked.

"A marathon?" Carl complained, "We don't have nearly enough space or time for that!"

"Oh?" Malevita asked. She clearly didn't even know how long a marathon was. "Then we'll make it a race. One sprinter from each team."

"There's a track up at fieldhouse," Roger mentioned.

"No!! Out here is just fine thank you!" she yelled.

"Okay, Malevita. Give us a minute to pick our runner," John requested.

"I have mine!" she pointed at a random three year old in the crowd. If all of her people truly were super humans with equal talent, it didn't matter who she picked. A little toddler would do just as well as a fit man.

"Huddle up team!" Joe shouted.

"Alright. Who's fast?" Marta asked.

"I guess I am," Mark offered.

"What do you mean 'you guess'? You either are, or you're not. Because I'm faster than the speed of light!" Carl boasted. But it was true, he was the fastest person John knew.

"Alright Carl, you go," Mark agreed. "I'll have my turn."

"Competitors, line up with me!" the impartial scorekeeper shouted. "You have to run one lap around the entire building, and the first person to reach me again wins! Ready, set, GO!"

The runners took off. Carl sprinted as fast as he could, bursting past the girl. *Boy, I am cookin'!* He thought. "Eat my dust!" he shouted victoriously as he ran, kicking dust up behind him.

"Faster girl!!!" Malevita shrieked. "Why are you so slow?"

"I'm saving up my energy," she responded. "The building is very large."

"Don't save up anything, just RUN!!" Malevita instructed.

And so she did. She was extremely fast, and made every person on the fieldhouse team hold their breath.

"Come on Carl!" Joe shouted.

He was starting to fall behind, but the support from his buddy pushed him to finish strong.

Carl crossed the finish line first by an inch.

"Yes! Way to go Carl!" Marisol shouted.

"WHAT???!! How did I lose?" Malevita was shocked.

Marta was too. She looked at John who smiled in return.

"Great job Carl," everyone congratulated.

Carl sat down on a rock, panting quickly and heavily. The girl had used her intelligence to determine that she should save her energy so she wasn't as exhausted as he was. But that cost her the win that Malevita so intensely desired.

"So what's the next event?" Rose asked.

"We get to pick," Alex answered.

"Art, music, or academics?" Meg questioned.

"Let's do academics. How about a history test? We'll send Tim no question for that one!" Marta encouraged.

"But who's going to make the test?" Danny asked.

"I know someone..." John smiled. "I'll be back soon."

~

CHAPTER 42

Chapter 42

Mr. Holland heard a knock on his front door. His immediate first thought was that a robber had come, but he looked out the window and saw one of his students. It was John. He opened the door.

"John! What brings you here on a Saturday night? Especially since you haven't been in school again for a few days!"

"I'm sorry Mr. Holland. I don't mean to bother you, but it's really important. I need you to make the hardest history test you can."

"Excuse me?"

"Can you make two copies of an extremely difficult history test? Please?"

"That's the strangest request I have ever heard from a student who hates history class," Mr. Holland pointed out.

"Will you please just do it? I promise to never misbehave in your class again!"

"Mr. John, you have a deal!"

~

But for Tim, the test clearly wasn't hard enough. He breezed through all of the questions and turned it in quickly. He had to wait a longer time for the other person to finish. It was a very old woman who had probably *lived* through half of the test questions, and he didn't know how fair that was. But despite that possible advantage, they got the scores back and Tim had received 100%. The woman had only missed one.

"I can't believe it! That's totally unfair! The test was too easy!" Malevita argued.

"Would you like to take it?" Rose asked genuinely.

Malevita stopped talking, her pale cheeks turning rosy.

"Great job Tim!" Marta ran up to him and gave him another quick hug before Malevita chose the next event.

"Here's a piece of music that two people from each team have to sight read. It's a duet," Malevita explained as she chose two random people from the crowd.

"Who wants to do this one?" Erin asked. She looked around and no one seemed to be volunteering. "Don't everybody jump at once!"

"We'll do it!" Adella stepped forward, grabbing Marisol's arm.

"We will?" Marisol asked startled.

"Yes. We're best friends, and we might not be world famous singers, but we've sang with each other before. I doubt anyone else in this group has really done that."

"It's true," Meg confessed.

"Yeah, I'm not a music guy," Danny agreed.

"Go for it!" John exclaimed.

The music started and Malevita's team sang first. The people's voices sounded like sweet nightingales humming a beautiful tune as they sang their individual parts. But when they had to sing together, their voices did not coalesce. They had outstanding solo voices, but they did not know how to sing together as a team. Their song ended and the music started over for Adella and Marisol. They both started to sing, always together, even throughout the solo parts. This helped their intonation and though their style wasn't amazing, their harmonies blended together perfectly, like peanut butter and jelly. The song ended and the scorekeeper announced that the fieldhouse team had won the third competition, giving them the third point they needed for the win.

"NOOOOO!" Malevita shrieked. "How did I lose???" She was so distraught and angry that she didn't notice when Rose snuck up and stole the ray out of her hands. Rose pressed the button that transformed everyone back to their normal selves.

"I think you're a little outnumbered," Rose smiled. She then pointed Malevita's ray at its creator and temporarily knocked her out. Danny and Mark tied her up and stood guard. They weren't going to let her go anywhere except the uninhabited and isolated red planet.

Marta ran over to John. "How did you know?" she asked. "How did you have so much confidence that we would win?"

"I'm no genius, but a team beats out any one person no matter who he/she is," he reasoned.

And Marta knew it was true. Even if these people were exceptionally good at everything, their fieldhouse team had great teamwork. And even if Malevita truly was an evil mastermind, their team could stop her.

"John! Come here for a minute. I have something to tell you," Meg called from her position guarding Malevita.

"I'll be back," he promised Marta and began walking over to Meg.

As Marta watched John placidly walk away, her gaze diverted over to Tim who was working hard on his laptop, already on to the next project. She suddenly realized that she was slowly walking over to him, and decided not to stop herself. "Already on to the next thing?" she teased.

Tim looked up from his laptop and met Marta's deep brown eyes with a slight crooked smile that warmed her nervous body. He quickly looked away, turning his computer screen to show her what he was up to. "It's my newest design," he declared.

Inside, Tim did three cartwheels when he saw Marta's mouth gape slightly open. She must have been amazed by his new sketch of a rocket, the Marth I.

"And what's this?" she asked, when she could finally get the words to come out of her mouth.

"The Marth I is a rocketship I am designing to bring Malevita to mars," he stated proudly.

"That's amazing!" Marta praised. "But how can... can we build this?" she questioned.

She said we! Tim thought excitedly. *She's in on the project!* "So you want to help, then?" he asked hopefully.

"Of course! I'm totally in. And I know John will be too."

"Oh," he muttered disappointedly, clearly intending for the project to just be between him and Marta.

"You know the rest of the team is going to be needed for this, right?" Marta asked. "Adella and Marisol will know about space suit materials, Alex can help with the tech, Mark and Meg with the piloting, and everyone else will definitely want to help with whatever they can. You know Rose, Roger, Danny, Erin, Carl, and Joe are in for whatever adventure that might come, even if it is on the red planet."

"I guess you're right..." Tim nodded in agreement.

"Like always," John commented as he jumped back into the conversation.

Marta asked Tim with her eyes if it was okay to show John the rocket.

He nodded and turned the laptop toward John. "I designed this to send Malevita where she belongs."

"Whoa!" John exclaimed, flabbergasted. He was too amazed to make a snappy comment about the name Marth I. "When do we get started?" he asked excitedly.

"As soon as possible," Marta replied, looking to Tim to see if this was plausible.

"Yes, the designing is done, so now we just have to get the supplies, build the rocket, do a trial run, fix the errors, design a space suit, and set the course for Mars."

"That's a pretty daunting list. Let's call over the team," Marta exclaimed.

~

CHAPTER 43

Chapter 43

"Watch out!!" Alex shrieked.

They had been building the rocket based off of Tim's design, and everything was going well. Until Danny accidentally sparked the wires and a large section of the rocket they had built so far combusted into flames.

"Aaaah!" Marisol jumped back, away from the flames.

Carl and Joe stood completely still, staring at the flickering flashes of fiery lights.

"Where's the fire extinguisher!?" Mark shouted to Roger, hoping he had one in the giant fieldhouse.

"Don't have one," Roger admitted anxiously.

"Who doesn't have a fire extinguisher in such an enormous and important building filled with technology fire hazards!!!???" Mark retorted with frustration.

While he was shouting his voice away, Meg looked for a hose. She found one and immediately subdued the metastasizing flames, revealing the melted and scarred metal.

Tim cautiously walked up to the rocket, examining the damage. "I think we're going to have to try take two," he suggested. "Any rocket that will combust into flames from the smallest spark will assuredly not make it farther than the roof of a building," he observed.

"I think you're right," Marta agreed. "We just need a heat resistant material."

"How about a fire resistant one?" Adella asked, holding up her invented fire, water, and extreme temperature resistant suits.

"That should do it," Alex agreed, taking the suit and trying to discover how to convert it into a metal.

Rose came running in with an exasperated look on her face. "Malev-" she started, then her attention diverted to the smell of smoky fire and her eyes started to sting and fill with water. "Why does it smell like smoke in here?" she asked.

"Let's just say that Marth II will be needed," Joe chuckled.

"What were you going to say about Malevita?" John asked.

"Oh yeah!" Rose rushed as the look of concern reappeared on her small face. "She's waking up! We need to do something about it before she escapes!"

"I'll help you out Rose," Danny offered. "I'm not much of a help here..."

"Yeah more of a hinderance actually," Carl pointed out.

"Carl!" Adella scolded.

"It's okay. He's right. I'll be better at watching over Malevita," Danny grinned and rubbed his hands together, following Rose into another room.

~

"Alright guys. In order to finish the Marth II before Malevita wakes up, we need teamwork," Marta declared. "Adella, Marisol, and Erin, I need you guys to work on the mastermind's space suit. Tim, Alex, Mark, and

Meg, you guys start on the Marth II. Carl and Joe, you guys go with Rose and Danny to guard Malevita. John and I will work on the logistics for the actual flight. You think we can do it?" she asked encouragingly.

"Let's get to work!" everyone agreed.

~

"So how long does it take to go to Mars exactly?" John wondered.

"This site says about 7 months, 14 for a round trip," Marta replied.

"But we don't need to worry about that. This shuttle has a one way ticket!" John added.

"Well, actually, I was thinking about that. Can we trust Malevita to be in the Marth II by herself? Knowing her, she could come up with something that would allow her to take over the entire solar system. Or destroy it..."

Marta waited in silence for John to reply.

After taking a few precious minutes to make a good decision, he finally spoke up. "You're right. We need people to ride with Malevita to Mars, to watch over her, and to make sure everything goes as planned with the Marth II. We need to draft a good team of people to make the journey, but still leave a good team here at fieldhouse for a mission control center."

"Yeah, that's a good idea. We're going to need people with certain strengths on both sides, so let's think about it. Let's partner up everyone with someone of similar strengths."

"Alright, well Carl and Joe is a no brainer. Adella and Marisol, too."

"How about Tim and Alex? Mark and Meg. Danny and... Rose?"

"Danny and Rose!! That's a *little* uneven," John criticized.

"Okay, good point. One is strong, the other is quick, and they're both needed. Let's do Roger with Danny, and Erin with Rose," Marta suggested.

"Sounds good. Let's write down who from each pair is staying and who's leaving," John got a piece of paper.

People on the Mission

Mark

Tim

Rose

Danny

Marisol

Carl

People staying in control center

Meg

Alex

Erin

Roger

Adella

Joe

"Looks great!" Marta agreed. Her smile suddenly faded.

"What's wrong?" John asked.

"I think we forgot somebody..."

"Oh, sorry! Who?" John asked.

"Us...I'll go," she offered.

"No way! I want to go! Rocket ships, aliens, and space! That's totally my kind of thing!" John shouted excitedly. "You have to let me go! And plus, you're needed in the mission control center back here to make sure everything runs smoothly."

Marta bit her lip in deep thought. She knew how much John wanted to go, and she had to admit, she was scared to go herself. But she didn't want to send John on a rocket to Mars with an evil mastermind. That plan just sounded like it had a very large potential for disaster. But he was right about somethings. She was needed back at the fieldhouse, and one of them had to be on the rocket to use their intelligent problem solving minds. It was extremely hard for her to make the decision, but with a tentative nod, she was sending her twin brother on a rocket to Mars.

~

CHAPTER 44

Chapter 44

"Put that there," Tim ordered, pointing to a spot on the Marth II.

Alex attached the small metal piece to the rocket.

"Wow, it's coming along great guys!" Marta exclaimed as she and John entered the room.

"How long 'till launch?" John questioned excitedly.

"We'll be ready for a test run in about a half an hour," Meg estimated, brushing the dust off of her jeans.

"Great. We'll check on the other people and will be back then. How long will the journey be?" Marta asked to see if this feat was truly possible.

"A normal rocket could complete the trek in about 7 months, but mine can do it in one."

"*Your* rocket?? You mean *ours,* don't you??" Mark snapped.

"You guys all did a great job and I'm really impressed so far. We'll be back in half and hour," Marta added as she and John left the room.

~

"How's the suit coming?" John asked. "Cause we're gonna need seven more!"

"John!" Marta scolded, elbowing his side. "I wasn't going to tell them yet!"

"Tell us what?" Erin asked suspiciously.

Marta glared at John, then sighed. "We can't trust Malevita to be in the rocket by herself. We are sending a team to Mars with her, and the others will stay back in fieldhouse to run a control center."

That was all that needed to be said. Adella's eyes widened with fear, and her mouth gaped slightly open. But she slowly walked over to Marta, placing a surprisingly warm hand on her shoulder. "I'll do whatever you need me to," she supported. "How many suits do we need?"

"Eight total, including Malevita's. Here's the list," John declared.

Marisol blinked a few times and looked back at the page. She was on the list to go on the mission. "I don't understand!" she whispered when she could finally find words. "Why am I on the mission list? I'm no help on Mars! I don't know a thing about space."

"That may be true, but we need your teamwork and communication skills," Marta explained.

"But is it safe? How will we know they're okay? I can't imagine being a planet away from you, Marisol! We've never even been a state away!" Adella protested.

"Oh, come on! It'll be great!" John exclaimed. "Haven't you ever imagined what the solar system really looks like?"

John just didn't understand. Marta knew exactly how Adella was feeling, but she had no words of comfort or advice. She couldn't convince Adella that everything would turn out fine when she hadn't even convinced herself yet.

~

"How's Malevita?" John asked Rose.

"Still snoring like a lawnmower," she replied, covering her ears with her small hands.

"Good," Marta nodded. "Tim is running a test run for the Marth II if anyone wants to come see it," she offered.

Carl, Joe, and Rose all looked at each other with fascination and eager hopes.

"I'll stay and stand guard. You guys can go," Danny volunteered. He looked rather relieved to not have to go back to the room with the rocket. Marta figured that he must have still felt responsible for the fire incident on the Marth I.

"Thanks Danny. You won't need to stand guard for that much longer anyway, because Tim's rocket is going to work, I know it is," Marta encouraged.

John eagerly led the others back to the rocket, where Tim, Alex, Mark, and Meg stood proudly.

"Is it ready for take off?" Carl asked.

Tim answered with the click of the big green button, and a deep rumbling ensued. The Marth II rose off the ground, shooting into the sky.

Mark and Meg had quarreled about who got to pilot the test run, but Meg won. She figured that she had no chance whatsoever of flying the real mission, so she figured that she should at least get to pilot the test run. And by saying that, Mark realized that she was probably right, so he reluctantly acquiesced.

Meg controlled the Marth II as it soared through the air. She carefully landed the rocket on the grass and everyone cheered. The Marth II was ready for the mission. But the question was, were *they* ready for the mission? Marta suddenly realized that half of the team didn't know the plan. She'd have to break the news.

"Great job, guys! The Marth II is a success! So now we need to talk about the logistics of this plan. John made it clear to me that Malevita could not be trusted on a rocket to Mars by herself, so..." she swallowed and took a deep breath to assuage her nerves. Her gaze darted to the ground; she couldn't look anyone in the eyes and tell them that she was sending them on a mission to Mars. "So we are sending people up to Mars with her to make the trip there, and come back alone and confident that Malevita has no way to destroy the universe."

Marta slowly looked up to see the team's reaction. To her surprise, Mark and Meg wore gleaming grins like little children seeing presents under a Christmas tree. Tim didn't look happy, but at least he didn't protest. Alex stared into the distance, gazing into a different world. Her head was already in space, dreaming. Rose had a confused look on her face, and Marta wondered if she even knew what Mars was. But nevertheless, when John told Rose she would be riding the rocket to outer space, she jumped up and down with excitement. Carl and Joe were always up for an adventure, and even though this one was a little daunting, they eagerly accepted. All in all, Marta was shocked. Everyone seemed relatively excited to participate in this audacious mission, whether they were the ones going to the dusty red planet or not.

~

Chapter 45

Danny intently watched Malevita like a hawk. He paid attention to the subtle rise and fall of her chest as she breathed in and out. Her eyes were closed lightly and he checked multiple times to make sure they were fully closed. Her pupils darted back and forth, up and down, most likely creating a dreamy vision she will may or may not remember. As he waited for the others to return, he wondered how long it would be until she would wake up. He also wondered if the rocket would be ready by then. Interrupting his thoughts, Malevita's left hand twitched slightly. He stiffened and took out his weapon, preparing for her to rouse. But before he could have expected it, Malevita's legs darted out, swiping Danny's legs out from under him. She swiftly rolled to her feet and ran away, a distinct escape plan already having formed in her complex structured mind.

~

But before Malevita could have gone far, Danny was already in the room with the rocket, telling the others about her escape.

Tim and Alex used their computer to locate the tracking device they had planted on her, just for this reason. Mark, Meg, Carl, Joe, Danny, and Rose all chased after Malevita, throughout the numerous rooms in the fieldhouse. Roger ran to his security base and activated the tasks in each room, hoping that it would delay Malevita. Each fieldhouse team member had an identification badge which allowed for them to pass through the challenges without participating. But Malevita would be slowed down by the daunting tasks.

~

She went to turn the door handle of the next door, but it did not budge. She pulled harder, kicking at the door hinge, hopelessly trying to escape. Sighing, she turned around to face the room she was trapped in. There was a small wooden table with a paper packet sitting on it. As she moved closer to the packet, she realized that it was a music score. The song was called "The Escape", depicting exactly what she needed to do. She lunged at the pages, intently desiring to tear them to shreds, but she managed to resist, knowing that they were her key through the locked door. Knowing what she had to do, but loathing it all the same, she opened her mouth and began to croak out the notes to the song.

~

"Tim to Chasers: I've found her!!! Room 39 and you won't believe it!!! It's on Roger's video screen here, and she's-- she's *singing*!!"

No one responded to Tim, but he didn't expect them to. They were probably doubling over with laughter. But he did know they would be on their way soon (as soon as they could gather themselves).

Roger watched the screen with Tim, biting his lip to retain his laughter. Malevita was trying to sing her way out of the room! The fact was, the music had nothing to do with the song or the notes. It was a hidden message.

The Escape - Noa Nysoum

Tim closely inspected the music displayed on Roger's screen as Malevita was singing. It took him a minute, but he figured it out. The musical alphabet only covered A - G, but the message had to have other letters in it. Tim discovered that if the note was a single quarter note, than it represented whatever letter name note it normally does on the staff. But if the note was a double eight note on D for example, then you would find the letter that takes D's position if you count again, starting with H. H I J **K**. K is fourth (where D was) and so the double eight note on D is K. Tim used this strategy for the triplets and sixteenth notes, counting three and four cycles past G. Finally, the quarter rests were spaces, and the half rest was a period. The final message was quite simple actually.

Look in floorboard in corner to find a key.

"She's right next to it!" Tim exclaimed.

"Next to what?" Roger asked.

"The key!!"

Roger smiled. "Very good Tim! I knew you were smart the moment you entered the fieldhouse on the first day of the competition."

Tim beamed with pride and wished Marta was there to witness his glory.

Though Tim was smart enough to see past the notes, Malevita failed to find the code that would direct her towards her key out of captivity.

~

Malevita was interrupted mid song by a group of brave and determined kids.

“Hello maestro!” Meg shouted as Danny and Mark closed in on her. Her face turned as red as a cherry tomato with a fluster of anger and embarrassment. Carl, Joe, and Rose darted around the room, both distracting her, and drawing out her energy as she chased them. It helped that she was already out of breath from singing. The boys tackled and tied her up to bring back to Marta and John. They would know what to do with her.

~

Chapter 46

Malevita woke up to find herself locked in a secure seat on the Marth II, wearing a spacesuit Adella designed. Next to her on the right was Danny with a tight nervous expression on his face. He wasn't looking forward to the long journey in a rocket going to a place he wasn't even sure truly existed. To Malevita's left was Carl, eagerly tapping his feet while watching a basketball game on his phone. Mark and Tim were seated in the cockpit, ready to control the rocket's take off. Meg had been right after all. Mark would be piloting the real mission. Rose, John, and Marisol were seated behind Malevita, Carl, and Mark, contacting Marta at the mission control base before take off. They had plenty of hydroponic supplies for food on their journey, and they had easy access to water thanks to Alex and Tim's invention; it was a machine that could pump extra hydrogen atoms to combine with the oxygen in the air to be converted into pure water. They had plenty of things to do, for most of the kids had piles of schoolwork to make up, and when they were not doing that, they would be communicating with the mission control base for the status back at the fieldhouse.

"Mark to Meg: How are we looking?"

"You seem pretty nervous and disheveled to me," she pointed out.

Mark grunted. "I meant the rocket! Are we ready for take off?"

"All systems are go," Marta reported. "Everybody okay?" she asked, clearly second guessing her decision to send John.

"Ready to roll," John replied, knowing that Marta's concern was directed towards him.

"Launching in 10, 9, 8, 7, 6..." Tim counted down as the rocket started to rumble. Danny ducked his head between his knees. Carl and Rose grinned. Mark held both of his hands on the controls. Tim crossed his fingers. Marisol closed her eyes, leaning back in her chair. Malevita scowled maliciously yet fearfully. She had the tiniest feeling of dread that the kids' insane plot might actually work, and she would be stranded on Mars. "5, 4, 3, 2, 1, BLAST OFF!!" Tim shouted as the Marth II exploded from the fieldhouse woods, blasting into the sky like a flash of lightning. Danny's head flew out from it's position between his knees, slamming into the headrest with the sudden motion. Rose flew up a little off of her seat, for the seatbelt was too small for her. She hovered in the air for a split second, then slammed back into her seat. It was a rough take off, but the Marth II was on its way to Mars.

~

Marta watched as the Marth II darted across the sky and was out of her vision faster than she could wave goodbye. She blinked and opened her eyes again, searching the sky for the rocket as if they would float down that second after a successful mission. But it didn't work that way. She wouldn't see John or Tim- or any of the others for two months. They would be the longest and loneliest two months of her life. She felt a tear slip out and roll down her cheek. Before she could wipe it away, she noticed Adella was tearing up as well. She and Marisol were the closest friends to each other that Marta would ever meet. Meg was gazing through the sky, also trying to find a trace of the rocket. She hopelessly slumped into a chair in front of a computer screen to try and hide her tears as well. After Mark saved her, and maybe even before then, he meant a lot to her. Joe seemed lost without his buddy Carl, and Roger was crying at the thought of his little daughter traveling to Mars. Erin and Alex were the only two members of the team who were still standing strong, and they were ready to do something about it.

“Hey guys! It’s alright,” Erin tried to lighten the mood. “We can talk to them through Marisol’s excellent system.”

“Yeah, and it’s not like we’ll never see them again!” Alex added. “Well, hopefully...”

Everyone groaned.

“That was not the right thing to say,” Erin whispered as she elbowed Alex. “Come on guys! We have it easy. It’s not in our hands anymore.”

“That’s what I’m afraid of,” Meg mumbled.

Silence ensued Meg’s dark comment.

Gathering courage and confidence in her twin brother and good friends, Marta broke the silence. “It’s up to them, and we know they’ll do great. Let’s call them now and see how they’re doing.”

“Control center to Marth II: How was take off?” Alex asked.

Marisol, head of communications, looked around the rocket. She was a little shaken up herself, and Danny was a bit green, but everyone else beared enormous grins. So far they were doing just fine. “Successful take off. Everyone is doing great. We’re all ready to do whatever it takes.”

“Whatever it takes to do what?” Joe asked cluelessly.

“To stop Malevita from destroying the universe,” John replied.

“No promises,” Malevita cooed.

~

Author Bio

Meet T Berry Jones

T Berry Jones is a fifteen year old high school student living in Pittsburgh, Pennsylvania. She got her inspiration for Masterminds when playing inventive games with her sisters. In addition to creative writing, she loves music, sports, science, and math. She loves learning about outer space and specifically Mars, but hasn't quite finished her design of the Marth rocket. T Berry Jones also enjoys reading fantasy books with her friends and is excited to add another book to the shelf.